THE GOLDEN ORRERY

SAGA OF A SICILIAN IN AMERICA

A NOVEL

By

Joseph Antinoro-Polizzi

AUSONIA PRESS

Library of Congress Cataloging in Publication Data

Antinoro-Polizzi, Joseph

THE GOLDEN ORRERY: Saga of a Sicilian in America
A NOVEL
by Joseph Antinoro-Polizzi-1st Ed.

ISBN: 978-0-9828075-1-4

1. Antinoro-Polizzi, Joseph 2011   2. Sicily, America
3. Immigration   4. Fiction 1907-1971
5. Baroque Architecture, Vincenzo Sinatra; Sir Anthony Blunt

Printed in the United States of America
    West Coast Printing FL
    111 Corporation Way/Venice, Florida 34285
    Cover Design by Katrishia Powell
    Cover Photograph: Federico Antinoro, circa 1908

Mechanical manuscript preparation/formatting by Norma Lee Rhines

Published by:

AUSONIA PRESS
Post Office Box 534
Tallevast, Florida 34270-0534

Second Printing 2012

This is a work of fiction. Names, characters, places and incidents are either products of the author's imagination or, if real, are used fictitiously.

This is the story of an ambitious
young man who leaves the
service of a Sicilian prince
and his true love
to find his future life and fortune
in America
and of
his grandson who returns
to Sicily many years later
to recapture the past

ORRERY: A mechanical device (model) of the solar system or planets revolving around the sun. Named after the fourth Earl of Orrery, Charles Boyle (1676-1731).

-Webster

ACKNOWLEDGMENTS

With special appreciation and gratitude

to

Alessandra De Stefanis

for

her gentle inspiration, many helpful
observations and suggestions, and
steadfast encouragement during every
phase of production of this work

Special thanks

to

Norma Lee Rhines

for typing and formatting the manuscript

DEDICATION

To the happy memory of
my
Uncle and Aunt,
John and Anna Puma
and my
Godparents,
Joseph and Amelia Incardona
who,
in many wonderful and
loving ways, ignited my
desire to write this story

"He who takes the new path rather
than the old, knows what he leaves
behind but not what will enfold"

– Italian proverb

TABLE OF CONTENTS

BOOK ONE

Book One

Part One
1907 - 1908

BEGINNINGS Prince Bronte had
  Noto, Sicily   provided one of his
      1907   carriages and drivers
to take Federico to the Ursuline convent
in an ancient quarter of the city. As he
peered out the small coach's window, the
young Sicilian was painfully aware his
momentous decision meant that for a very
long time, or perhaps never again, would
he see the gathering places of his youthful
years—the charming piazzas, with their
playful fountains and open-air cafes, the
lovely churches approached by majestic
steps, the tidy green parks with statuary
fronting the grand municipal buildings.

It was approaching seven, the "Hour of Enchantment." The lowering sun, unfettered from the pitiless summer sirocco, cast long, golden-rose beams over the landscape, gilding the ornamental features of the elegant edifices at the center of the city. These late seventeenth and early eighteenth century baroque marvels stood as exuberant, theatrical testaments to Sicilian resiliency—the will to endure and rebuild after natural calamity.

From ancient times, the majestic but menacing presence of Mount Etna— with its eruptions once believed to emanate from the fiery forge of Vulcan, and catastrophic earthquakes from the futile rumblings of Typhon attempting to escape his petrous imprisonment— never failed to remind the islanders of the power and capriciousness of Nature and the fragility and brevity of human existence.

Centuries of countless invasions and conquests, exploitation and oppressive rule took an even greater toll on the Sicilian psyche. Sadly, even national political unification—with all its stirring rhetoric and romance, as well as horrors of rebellion and revolution—had failed to deliver on some of the promises (or expectations) of regime change, and, in the long run, proved to be a rather mixed blessing for both Sicily and the Mezzogiorno* or southern part of the mainland. Ruled and administered as "The Kingdom of the Two Sicilies," these two regions comprised the largest and wealthiest of the Italian states before unification. However, their subsequent impeded development—the so-called "Southern Question"—had drawn the attention of thinkers and writers, politicians and agents of change who either extolled or condemned their "picturesqueness" and traditionalism. Meanwhile, omnipotent

---

* "Land of the Noonday Sun"

3

Nature continued to be unmerciful in still other ways—severe droughts, crop failures and pestilences, eventually driving many inhabitants to utter despair. Little wonder that many Sicilians believed they were "born old, wise and worried."

Although he wasn't completely insulated from these present realities of *"miseria,"* Federico never fully subscribed to the fatalistic notion of *"destino."* He believed he was made of another clay. *"Volontá"* or "Will" would have been the motto inscribed at the center of his shield or escutcheon. Perhaps this was what was leading him to seek a new life and fortune in America. It had been a difficult decision, filled with doubts and misgivings. Nevertheless, he had finally convinced himself it was the right thing to do. He was now twenty-two years old and life seemed to be passing him by.

Like many others, Federico had succumbed to the stories and tales about the fabled land, America. Those less well-positioned or fortunate than he, however, were seeking a release from impossible situations, stemming from not only inimical natural forces, but from poverty and lack of opportunity brought on by excessive land fragmentation and population pressure. His decision was not one fashioned out of desperation. He would be leaving a relatively secure existence. In some curious and perhaps paradoxical way, his attachment to a relatively stable and still prospering traditional princely household played a part in fostering his present outlook and his desire for adventure and fortune.

In his childhood years, Federico (or "Fede," as he was affectionately called) was expected to carry out little tasks around the busy workaday palace service quarters—running errands, relaying messages, assisting with feeding and currying the horses. Ever since his middle adolescent years, however—shortly after his primary education was complete—Federico had served Prince Bronte ably and faithfully, first as a junior administrator and then eventually as one of the senior stewards of his vast estates, including a brief stint as a manager at one of his vineyards in the far western part of the island near Marsala. Federico was smart, well-spoken and tactful; he had good instincts, an astute business sense and management style, qualities which the prince recognized very early on.

Don Fabrizio Bronte, Prince of Terranova-Chiaravalle, was a handsome, tall and imposing forty-five year-old man with a copious mane of slightly graying blond hair, steel blue eyes and fair complexion.

Whereas, on the one hand, many members of his social stamp slumbered indolently under a heraldic canopy of ancestral honors and privileges—subscribing neither to esoteric or "excessive" learning, nor, heaven forbid, any form of "practical" instruction—he, on the other hand, had been schooled from childhood by demanding, erudite tutors in the *artes liberales* or liberal arts, especially an updated, modern version of the medieval *quadrivium* of arithmetic, geometry, music and astronomy; upon entering his twenties, he had pursued serious and weighty studies both in the sciences, as well as the classics and humanities at the University of Palermo and the University of Rome on the mainland.

The prince did not suffer unctuous flattery or stand on excessive ceremony.

An agnostic, he nevertheless reverently observed religious conventions. Within his social milieu, he was regarded as an enlightened man who carried his august titles with dignity and a grave sense of *noblesse oblige*. Without relying on the ineffectual (and often oppressive) national government for any support, he had attempted, with some success, to restructure and reclaim a portion of his unproductive latifundial land for the benefit of a few of the landless. He had even divested himself of the ownership of a large sulphur mine because he could not renovate its operation sufficiently to reduce what he deeply lamented were horrific and intolerable working conditions, especially for very young children known as *carusi*.

Of course, for these attitudes and attempts at change, he was subject, at times, to *sotto voce* criticism and mistrust, perhaps even hatred, by other *signori* who feared and abhorred social subversion. He was, however, unassailable and untouchable, from even more sinister forces, by virtue of the great antiquity of his many noble titles and, not insignificantly, his generous philanthropies to high culture, both in Noto and the island's glorious capital, Palermo. Over the centuries, the prince's family with its motto, *"Virtute securus"* ("Secure through virtue"), enjoyed pre-eminence in several dynastic annals, most notably, *The Golden Book of Sicilian Nobility.*

As customary among the gentry, the prince maintained several dwellings: a seldom visited ancestral castle in Agrigento, a small seaside villa near Catania, two country houses (actually, vast working farms), his *Casa* or palace in Noto (his principal and favorite home), and an elegant townhouse in Palermo. He dutifully took up residence in the last according to the expectations of the seasonal social calendar. However, being a serious intellectual and disciplined man, he avoided, as much as politely possible, the seemingly endless ritual amusements: the round of lavish balls and theatre parties, the promenades in Villa Giulia, the parading in elegant flower-bedecked carriages, the viewing of fireworks from yachts anchored at the Lido, the sumptuous dinners and banquets, and the easily addictive pastimes of card-playing, gambling and other games of chance.

Over the decades, new attitudes and material inventions had made inroads, altering and even, at times, unraveling or displacing some of these customs or traditional diversions. Without fail, however, the prince vigilantly eluded any possible mention by the so-called modern press of his participation in these *divertimenti*, old or new. For someone of his distinguished lineage, society news no longer had the cachet of much earlier times and generations. In his opinion, publicity now chased too many of the newly arrived, and doted over vapid or flamboyant tastes and frivolous comings-and-goings and conspicuous consumption of a baronry and upstart rich bourgeoisie, neither really loved nor admired.

Truth be told, the prince much preferred a stimulating conversation or literary dialogue at one of the few remaining select salons; an interesting lecture at the still active scientific society; or just a simple late afternoon visit to play chess and sup with one of his noble friends who might be spending a few days reviewing the care and keep of enamel-green groves of rare oranges at a country villa in nearby Bagheria.

Unquestionably, however, the paramount draw of the beautiful royal city was its rich musical culture. Much to his liking, Palermo provided the prince with the perfect venue for establishing and generously supporting a performance forum for talented young artists and promising composers and their small orchestral and operatic ensembles.

The prince had read his Plato and his Plutarch, his Macchiavelli, as well as his Darwin. He was conversant with the American, British and continental sociopolitical theories and aims, and those that had been expounded by his countrymen, Count Cavour and Mazzini, at the time of the *Risorgimento** when he himself was a mere infant. Nevertheless, he kept his personal views of governance *in petto*—"close to the vest"—and remained distant or aloof from any machinations or intrigues. He no doubt took instruction from the old admonition of Pythagorus—*"Fastineto a fabis"* or "Abstain from beans," meaning "avoid the ballots," that is, elections or the public arena of politics. Of course, if he had ever so desired, he could certainly have

---

* the movement for Italian unification
and the eventual establishment of a republic

wielded considerable influence, political or otherwise, behind the scenes, simply by virtue of who he was.

At home in his beloved *Casa*, the prince's favorite leisure pursuit was surveying the heavens from his observatory. In a moment of inspiration, it was also his habit to depart his telescope and the silent dances of the spheres, and repair to the music room. There he would tune the antique *cembalo* and play late into the evening the compositions of Bach and the rich sonoral and lyrical contrapuntal works of the Italians, especially the Neapolitans and the Sicilian Scarlattis.

As for the outdoors, he took some pleasure in the cultivation of rare and exotic flowers and varieties of palms and cacti in his garden. He found hunting unattractive and rather distasteful on humane grounds. He preferred instead, a morning or early evening walk accompanied by his gentle greyhounds or, for a change of pace, a brisk ride astride one of his favorite spirited and nimble-footed chestnut Arabians, along the undulating borders and paths of his vast, golden wheat fields,

Federico's initial vacillation, coupled now with the press of time of his quickly approaching scheduled departure, made it virtually impossible for someone to be trained to take over his duties at the palace. He deeply regretted this situation and felt that he was abandoning the prince, the gentle man, who, for as long as he could remember, had made life safe and pleasant for him, a foundling.

Although Federico recognized that the prince always treated him kindly and with fairness, in fact, up to this point, he

had inhabited a rather strange netherworld between life in the servants' quarters and his rather privileged involvement in much of the everyday management of the business affairs of the prince. At best, this stewardship afforded only a tenuous association with the sacrosanct, jealously private life of culture and leisure, genteel manners and white-gloved liveried servants in the elegant palace. Federico, however, was keen, sensitive and impressionable, internalizing much of what he observed, even at a distance. And, despite this somewhat peculiar marginal existence, he always felt a personal closeness to the prince, both his benefactor as well as his employer.

Ever the quintessential gentleman, the prince responded to difficult, and even highly charged issues, with impeccable courtesy and an air of distant, almost Olympian reserve; he was always supremely adept at concealing his true feelings. However, when Federico revealed his plans for an imminent departure to America, the prince, under the guise of surprise and astonishment, attempted, but failed somewhat, to veil a certain disappointment, perhaps even hurt. At the same time, it seemed he wanted to tell Federico something, but just couldn't bring himself to do it. Federico felt at a loss and tristful in this moment of impending separation, but he too stifled his true and somewhat complicated, emotions.

. . . The ancient walls of the Ursuline convent were coming into view. Federico gazed once more at the beautiful object which the prince, rather impulsively, had taken from its prominent place atop his bureau plat and then given to him as he embraced him and bid him goodbye. As the carriage neared the convent, Federico carefully returned the memento to its velvet-green coverlet.

The gift was truly unusual—an intricately wrought miniature gold orrery, an object which Federico had often secretly admired whenever he met with the prince in his elegantly appointed study.

When the prince gave it to Federico, he had said —

"May this remind you of me, Federico. Like the planets circling in their orbits, may it bring you around and back to us, with all your dreams fulfilled."

Everyone knew that the prince loved to observe the heavens, spending countless hours in his small rooftop observatory, reached directly by a winding wooden staircase from his study.

Federico was struck that the prince

had intuited the object of his admiration, and he realized how precious and personal this departing gift truly was.

. . . Now, as the driver pulled back on the reins, the graceful horse whinnied and the elegant little equipage came to a gentle halt. Holding the precious gift close to his chest, Federico stepped down hastily from the shiny black carriage.

THE CONVENT Federico reached
1907 and pulled the chain, ringing the tiny bell at the convent gate. From a small grated window somewhere in the courtyard he heard an angelic voice say, *"Sia lodato, Gesu Cristo"* — "Jesus Christ be praised" – to which he responded, *"Sempre sia lodato,"* that is, "May He always be praised." "Oh, Federico," said the nun, recognizing his voice, "Rosalia is anxiously waiting for you. She has been keeping us all excited to see you and to hear of your plans." As she came to open the gate, leading him

inside, she continued, "Is it really so, Federico? Are you intending to leave us and go to America?" "Yes, sister," he replied, "It is really coming to pass." "O God be with you, Federico. Wait here in the little room next to the chapel. I will get Rosalia for you."

Federico now faced the most difficult part of his departure, to say goodbye to the young woman he loved dearly, and to assure her that as soon as he had established himself in the new land, he would call for her.

Rosalia had been orphaned at the tender age of three. Her mother, a poor widow, had drowned while washing clothes in the river. A distant relative, friendly with the Ursuline Sisters of the Holy Family Convent, had sought their help in caring for and educating her. At the time, many of the sisters were from families of the nobility—a not uncommon reality in Sicily—and they had taught Rosalia many of the traditions and courtesies of their stratum; consequently, she possessed a distinctive degree of culture and refinement. She was now sixteen years of age.

Rosalia was no exception to the fact that many of the children of the poorer classes were often more beautiful than those of the patricians who intermarried over generations within restricted kinships. She was a Greek Sicilian type–slight, with smooth, pale ivory complexion, large, piercing, almond-shaped green eyes and auburn hair. Her face, with its delicate thin nose and high cheekbones, seemed chiseled from illumined alabaster.

Federico loved looking at her. She reminded him, in some ways, of the women depicted on the priceless antique vases he had admired at the national archaeological museum in Naples while on a brief business trip with the prince. At the time, the rather pretentious young museum guide, not recognizing the prince, had been quick to inform them both that these vases and other exquisite antiquities from Pompei and Herculaneum had been originally housed in the great palace of the Bourbons at Portici, the summer resort town below Mount Vesuvius. In his affected voice and with mannered gestures, he had continued to explain that, after many decades, these and other treasures had been transported *in pompa magna*, that is, in a procession of great display and ceremony, to this present impressive dwelling in the royal city of Naples.

All this was certainly no news to the prince. First of all, he, a man *multarum literarum*—a very learned man—did not need any such instruction. He had a comprehensive knowledge of classical history and art, and in fact, had visited the museum and studied its extraordinary collection many times before. But even more to the point, not only had his ancestors enjoyed many years of close friendship with the family of Maurizio Emanuele di Lorena, the prince of Elboeuf, who had initiated the excavations at Herculaneum in the eighteenth century, but his own paternal grandparents had actually been present at this momentous 1822 event. Among the cherished keepsakes he preserved in his study was a signed engraving by Daudet commemorating the magnificent occasion. Somewhat amused, yet ever reserved and polite, he never made any mention of this to the pompous functionary.

Rosalia rushed into the room, breathless. "Federico, I hope I haven't kept you waiting long. I was in the garden with Sister Agnes. We were picking flowers for the altar and saying the rosary as we went along." Lightly touching his shoulder, she placed a fragrant, lilac-shaded Dianthus—a Mediterranean clove pink—in his lapel.

"The day seemed like an eternity. I have looked for every distraction to keep from counting the hours and minutes until you would come." "I know how you feel, Rosalia, it has been the same for me. However, knowing that this would be the last time I would see you, for the Good Lord knows how long, I have been troubled and perplexed. Dearest, you know I am not doing this—leaving our beautiful island and going to America—because of any deep discontent or silly caprice. Certainly, if we were to marry and live here, the prince, ever so kind to me, would keep me in his employ. Although we would not be rich, we would be comfortable and secure. But, as I've told you before, I just have this desire to find myself and our future, as well, in some new place. Is it foolish? Do you understand? Do you forgive me?"

"Federico, it is not foolish, there is nothing to forgive. I know you're doing this for us. We both were born to sorrows here—my dear mother's tragic death, your own uncertain beginnings. I trust "La Madonna." She will look after you. I know that sincerely in my heart. After all, we mustn't forget, it was at her May procession we first met."

"What is that you are holding in that lovely green cloth, Federico?" "It's a parting gift from the prince—it's an orrery. It shows mechanically how the planets revolve around the sun. I'll never be able to forget the manner and sentiment with which he gave it to me. The prince has been almost like a father to me. I feel that I am letting him down, abandoning him." "No, No, Federico—that isn't so!"

Looking closely at the gold object, Rosalia exclaims, "Oh, isn't it beautiful!" Federico points to it, making it move.

"See, Rosalia, at the center is the sun. While I am far away, I will think of myself as one of these planets. You, my dearest, will always be like the sun, the center of my thoughts." Federico then tenderly kisses Rosalia's forehead and clasps her hand tightly. She touches his cheek. "I promise I will write soon and often." "And I as well, Federico, my treasure."

Federico quickly takes his leave. Tearful and trembling, Rosalia seeks out Sister Agnes, her music teacher and favorite companion, who is still in the garden. She is unaware that Federico is fighting back tears too as he touches the Dianthus she gave him and rushes out the gate to the waiting carriage.

Later, as darkness fell on his little room in the palace service wing, Federico pressed the delicate blossom, "the flower of poets," between the pages of his black leather prayer book.

THE DEPARTURE The day of 1907 departure came upon Federico before he knew it. He was to leave by mid-morning and had yet to say his goodbyes to several of the palace workers and staff, many of whom he had known since childhood and were like family to him. One by one they came to give him an embrace and wish him well. Some asked him to look up a friend or relative who lived in one or another American city. Federico politely acknowledged each request but knew that he would probably have difficulty just getting himself around, given his rather limited English. He had had some opportunity to learn and speak the language a few times when English visitors and friends came to the palace, either on business or for extended stays for relaxation and pleasure and to "see the sights."

One person whom Federico especially cherished was anxiously waiting for him. She appeared sad and concerned. This was Mariannina, the cook, who had served the prince's family for more than thirty years. Widowed at a very young age with one child, a daughter, she had, in fact, spent most of her adult life in the kitchen and the adjacent vegetable and herb garden. Except for an occasional trip to Noto's central market or to the main piazza to attend a special holiday celebration or pageant, rarely did she venture very far into town to visit a relative or friend, or even a doctor, for that matter. Yet, despite this simple and seemingly humdrum existence, she had a jovial spirit and spritely manner, always exuding a love of life and of the people surrounding her.

Federico hugged her tightly and assured her he would be all right. Mariannina had always been concerned that Federico was too thin and fragile and did not eat enough. True, as a little fellow, he was terribly finicky. In his adolescent years, however, he relished everything she set before him and the others, and, as a result, he had filled in his tall, large-chested frame, developing in time, into an impressive, strong, strapping figure. His recent neatly trimmed moustache now gave him a more mature, rather dashing appearance. Whenever he stood in bright sun, his closely cropped sandy-brown, wavy hair appeared streaked with reddish tints, never failing to give an attractive coloring and animation to his countenance.

Certainly, it wasn't just Mariannina's concern for his nourishment or physical well-being that Federico appreciated. Rather, it was all her loving ways. For as long as he could remember, she had been, in many respects, almost like a mother to him. (Her very beautiful daughter, Viviana, who served as a maid in the palace, had also cared for him, but only for a very short while before she abruptly left Sicily to live with relatives and seek work in Naples.)

However, of Mariannina's many endearing qualities, Federico especially cherished her gifts as a raconteur and sage. Though tiny in stature, she always seemed larger-than-life when she assumed the role of storyteller.

Mariannina was not formally educated. She was, however, a living treasury of Sicilian oral folk culture and everyday practical wisdom. In the early evening, it was her pleasant custom to entertain a little company of young and old alike, gathered around her under a shady tree or in a cozy, out-of-the-way service portico of the palace. In a highly dramatic fashion—with exaggerated facial expressions and gestures—she would regale her rapt audience with colorful legends of the Crusaders and Paladins, their chivalrous deeds, their passionate loves, as well as many other fanciful yarns and fables about mythical giants, magical animals and the bewitching loomings and phantoms of the *Fata Morgana* along the coast of Sicily.Predictably, at some point, she would interrupt her engaging story at a cliff-hanger; then she would say, with a mischievous twinkle in her eye—"It is getting late, I'll have to finish tomorrow evening."

One short moral tale Federico often recalled was her account of Adam and Eve's introduction to new sources of sustenance after their fall and banishment from Paradise, the wondrous place where once they had enjoyed the luscious fruits of many beautiful trees. When God's ministering angels came to earth, they brought the unhappy exiles what they judged to be the "perfect food": an egg. The couple dutifully ate it but expressed no particular pleasure; in fact, they complained that it was tasteless! So, on their next visit, the angels instructed them to eat the egg *con sale*, that is, "with salt." They quickly complied, to their everlasting delight.

Without fail, Mariannina would then brightly add a little instructive coda or two to this tale, saying: "See, now you know how to answer the age-old question, 'What came first—the chicken or the egg?' And, remember too the old saying, 'If your life is boring, spice it up!'"

Just as Federico was about to take his things to leave, old Monsignor de Florio appeared at the door. For many years, he had been the chaplain of the prince's family; presently, he was in a kind of semi-retirement, assisting the young curate of a nearby church.

Stooped by severe arthritis, the

elderly priest had lost his once impressive height and bearing; his immaculate and perfectly pressed soutane accentuated his now very thin and fragile frame. Despite this visible wear of illness and time, his delicate facial features and refined mien still spoke eloquently of his younger years and former self. His warm and amiable disposition was reflected in his soft, cultivated voice, beseeching, all-knowing eyes and kindly gaze.

The monsignor had known Federico from his infancy and had instructed him at the time of his reception of first communion. He had taken this occasion, in fact, to introduce him to Dante, by way of the supreme poet's lovely cantos of the "Paradiso." Now, with a somewhat oblique allusion to his deeply revered versifier, he said to Federico—

"*Caro figlio*, (Dear son) no matter what life brings you in your new land, always remember your origins, and cherish and nurture your precious gift of faith."

Placing a rosary in Federico's hand, the elderly cleric then gently embraced and blessed him, adding—

"Whenever you pray this, remember me, Federico."

And with that, he quietly departed.

At this point, Federico felt more confident about his decision. He had received a blessing on his venture from the venerable prelate. The wise sibyl, his beloved Mariannina, had given him a savory recipe: he was going to America to add "salt" to his future life.

. . . As the caleche exited the gate of the palace courtyard, Federico looked back and saw the prince peering from behind the lace curtains of one of the tall windows of the *piano nobile.*

The sights, sounds and sensations
of the train ride to Messina would soon
put Federico into a quasi-dreamlike
state. Settling back in his rather stiff
green-velvet upholstered seat with his
small trunk of belongings shelved above,
he adjusted the open window to reduce
the smoke and black soot entering the
compartment. Here and there along the
way, he could see others less privileged,
trudging along, some on donkey carts
or mules, others walking, half-bent over,
carrying little children, or laden with the
meager and humble worldly possessions
they were taking to their new life. All
seemed to be dressed with layers upon
layers of clothing, a wise precaution
perhaps, since they would be arriving in a
climate so unlike that to which they were
accustomed.

Federico found the scene sad and
troubling. He pondered what would force
a people from a part of the world that had

such a rich history to take such desperate measures. What had caused such a fall from former greatness? Was this the fate of all civilizations? He asked himself – "Am I, in a way, just another pawn of some great mysterious process?"

The port at Messina was crowded with groups of people huddled here and there. Some were attempting to queue up in order to pass through a narrow ship entry point. Officious uniformed guards were pointing this way and that, while a spectacled physician in a long white coat, an iridologist, was performing a random check of the eyes of some about to board. Federico faintly overheard the doctor informing a very dejected-looking young man that the examination of his eyes revealed a serious hernia that had to be remedied before he could obtain passage.

Given his refined appearance and bearing, Federico merely received a brief perfunctory glance and, without any other delay, was waved on to the waiting vessel.

As the small ship began to cross the notoriously dangerous strait heading toward Naples, Federico was reminded of the legendary Aeneas, who, in order to continue his journey unharmed in this very part of the sea, had been warned to course his barque away from Scylla, the many-headed monster, and Charybdis, the thundering whirlpool. Federico hoped that he himself would be able to steer a safe passage between his personal ambition and capricious fortune. Would his optimism and will prevail over any obstacles along life's way?

Federico mused—"Was it not true that the great mother-goddess, Venus, had sought Jupiter's protective blessing upon her son, Aeneas, and his journey to reach 'the fertile land of *Ausonia*' or Italy?"

Now, he wondered, would the mother he had never known, look favorably and prayerfully, from wherever she might be, upon his quest, *his* journey to America?

That night, the fabled howling and hissing of the fearsome monster and the roar of the watery vortex would have been gagged by the all-too-real wailing and weeping of many of the passengers. It was a dirge Federico would never be able to erase from his memory.

SETTING SAIL Under the yellow-violet shadows of imperious Vesuvius brooding with spiraling smoke, the mole of Naples was sheer frenzy this particular morning. Literally hundreds were milling about, in a cacophony of different dialects, a seeming re-enactment of the biblical Tower of Babel.

As Federico disembarked, a painterly tableau appeared within his view:

near the shore to the west, fishing boats and other little pleasure crafts with colorful sails were coming and going; on the jetty itself, vendors of every description were hawking hot foods for the moment, as well as fruits, preserved meats, cheeses, and other non-perishables for the long ocean crossing; several brightly clad musicians were gaily playing their instruments, with an endearing curly-headed little boy singing his heart out; some nuns wearing large, unusually shaped white wimples were dispensing assorted items of aid and succor; *scugnizzi* or street urchins were searching for a lost *soldo* or copper on the pavement, or trying to cajole some sympathetic soul to gift them one; a small, elegant assembly of men with their valets, and women seeking shade under their dainty parasols—most probably English or American—had their lackeys pushing heavy trunks or some crated art treasure toward a nearby ship; and what could only be described as a "lady of charity," a noble woman, richly but somberly dressed, was devoutly accompanying a surpliced old priest and his ascetic-looking acolyte as they were giving benedictions and baptizing infants and other children who had as yet not been admitted formally into the life and grace of Holy Mother Church.

As Federico stepped forward, he noticed a spider-thin, bizarrely dressed woman with dark, kohl-rimmed eyes, a gypsy fortune-teller, trolling the crowd for business. Quickly advancing toward him, she blurted out loudly and boldly in dialect, "*Signù*, I can tell from your pale countenance that you long for your rosy love. Is it not true?" Stunned by her remark, Federico pretended not to have heard her, saying, "Good woman, please let me pass." The wizened old woman persisted – "Remember this, young gallant, I tell you that as you grow older and older, you will get richer and richer!" To avoid any further embarrassment, Federico quietly acknowledged her, placed a coin in her outstretched hand and walked away quickly. After another brief medical examination—answering some general health questions and a perfunctory view of his posture, hands and face—Federico ascended the gangplank. Within a short while, the foreign registered steamship cut moorings, ready to embark. Federico was admitted to his cabin where he hoped he eventually could catch up on the sleep he had lost during the mournful passage from Messina.

As the ship propelled seaward from the mole, Federico returned to the deck. He could see those remaining behind on the wharf waving white handkerchiefs until they eventually disappeared into the distance. From someplace down below, he could hear faint chatter and some melodic measures softly strummed on a mandolin.

Federico was familiar with the saying associated with *"Napoli nobilissima,"* the aristocratic city of enchanting beauty—"See Naples and die." Now, he mused, Naples was the city to see before finding *life*, a new life, that is, in America.

As he fell asleep that night, he pondered what the gypsy had said to him; he asked himself – "How had she conjured a 'rosy' love?" And of her prediction, "Was she just making a good guess, given the circumstances, or did she possess some truly genuine prophetic gift?"

Storms on the Mediterranean Sea were often fierce and dangerous, sometimes deadly. Federico hoped that Aeolus, the Father of the Winds, would be kind and that he would not have to experience one. Fortunately, it was the period before the heavy seasonal rainfalls and blustering wind patterns, and the voyage went smoothly without incident. Along the journey, Federico viewed the sleek and graceful, frolicking dolphins accompanying the ship as friendly and bléssed omens.

After the stop at Gibraltar, the entry into the Atlantic was both awe-inspiring and intimidating. Federico wondered how ships, however large, could stand up to the powers of such enormous natural forces. He thought about those intrepid explorers, such as his own countrymen, and how they had ventured where no one would have ever contemplated going. By comparison, his daring, if one could even call it that, seemed less than consequential.

Nevertheless, here he was on the Great Sea that, for several hundred years, had served as the artery for the transmission of western civilization and its peoples to the New World and all it promised. Federico saw himself humbly as one tiny link in a long chain, in a great drama, as one actor among many.

THE CROSSING At the departure in 1907 Naples, Federico had casually introduced himself to two young men who were also travelling cabin-class. Rinaldo Marselli was a sculptor who had trained and worked at the renowned Chiurazzi foundry in Naples. He was headed for Washington where his two uncles, also sculptors, were already working with other artisans— masons, stonecutters and *stuccatori* or workers-in-stucco—decorating a number of government buildings. He had made the crossing once before but had returned home to see his mother who was nearing death. "Now," he told Federico, "I am going to America for keeps. There is so much work there and I think I have fallen in love with a pretty girl who lives in Baltimora."

43

Francesco de Angelis also hailed from Campania, from a little picturesque mountain town just beyond Salerno that looked down upon the Sele plain and Paestum, an early Doric Greek settlement famous for its marvelous temples and celebrated, from ancient times, for its twice-blooming roses. He had been away for quite a while, studying music composition in Rome; he was going to Pittsburgh, Pennsylvania to assume a position in the music department of a small college. His older brother, a journalist, had preceded him some time earlier to work for a fledgling Italian American newspaper in California. Like Rinaldo, Francesco had made the journey once before to explore career possibilities.

The three young men took a liking to one another quickly, perhaps in great part because of the perspectives they shared as southerners. Each day they sought one another's company—for meals, for a friendly card game of *scopa* and just to talk, often for hours on end, about their hopes and dreams, as well as fears and misgivings, regarding their future in a new land.

Rinaldo was somewhat of a *bon vivant*, cheerful and lively, with a happy-go-lucky and rather expansive personality. Francesco, on the other hand, was friendly but quiet and pensive, a much more introspective type. Both young men found Federico's personal story interesting and unusual, certainly very different from their own upbringing. (Unknown to Federico at this time, these new-found friendships would endure for his entire lifetime; in fact, in just a few years, these young men and their spouses would be the godparents of his children.)

One afternoon all three were made

glaringly aware of the plight of their fellow countrymen traveling below, when on Francesco's suggestion, they went on to the deck area assigned to the passengers in steerage. It was the least desirable region of the deck where some crew members also relaxed or carried out certain unpleasant and messy tasks, such as butchering. Those in steerage were allowed here, just a couple of hours or so each day, to breathe fresh air and to catch a little sunshine.

The trio looked forward to enjoying some of the music played by passengers who were carrying instruments with them—guitars, violins, accordions, and mouth-organs, but mainly mandolins. They anticipated that, in a rare moment of merriment and abandon, some of the passengers would choose to dance, thereby adding to the entertainment.

At first, some of the passengers were wary to associate with their perceived betters, these young *signori* from cabin class, but most, with customary Italian cordiality, even in these circumstances, welcomed the young visitors and offered them something from the modest provisions they had taken on board.

Two men soon came forward, one of whom began to complain about the crew, saying that they looked upon the steerage passengers with contempt as social inferiors. He said, "These are brutish people; they are hard, they have hairs in their hearts." They then proceeded to take the trio into the steerage itself, the area of the ship near the rudder or below the water line.

It was an unforgettable Stygian scene: dank and dark, suffocating and foul-smelling, cramped quarters of crude wood berths, devoid of any provision for comfort or privacy whatsoever. Rinaldo forced back tears and queried, "How can you endure this?" One of the men said,

"*Signù*, what is our choice? To return to starvation and deprivation? No, it is better we drown or perish in this ocean water than eat the dirt and humiliation of poverty. Maybe someday, I pray, our children or their children will vindicate our suffering."

As they exited the dreary quarters, some curious youngsters began to gather around them. All of a sudden, there was screaming and wailing, "Look," shouted a woman, "she jumped overboard with her baby!" No sooner had she said that, a distraught man whizzed by yelling, "Carla, Carla, *Diu Benedettu*, what have you done?" And within a second, he jumped into the water after her. Before Federico and his friends or any others could rush topside to alert the officers, the family disappeared into the sea.

Inquiries among the passengers revealed a story that unfortunately—in one form or another—would be repeated many times over in the drama of emigration. Apparently, this poor soul had passed through the medical exam with her condition of trachoma going formally unregistered. When questioned by the doctor's assistant, she had given an excuse, saying that her eyes were merely irritated by her crying and tears at departing from her family. During the trip, however, as her condition worsened, she became convinced that she would be rejected entry and deported, thereby depriving her husband and child of a new better life. Other women who had befriended her had observed that she was constantly depressed at having left behind her ailing elderly parents and siblings whom she loved and already missed very much.

That evening Federico completed his first letter to Rosalia. He expressed how much he missed her and how much he loved her. He recounted all the fascinating aspects so far of his trip, and gave descriptions of his new friends. However, he decided it would be both kind and prudent not to tell her about this tragic episode, one he wished he had never experienced.

During the days that followed, Federico perceived things in the atmosphere that were changing: the luminosity of the sky, the shading of the waters, the cresting and flow of currents, the unusual formation and coloring of clouds. Like the elements, he also was experiencing change, an anxiety mixed with a building sense of expectation and renewal. He thought to himself—*"Ah, America, chissá che futuro mi aspetta!"* ("Oh, America, who knows what future awaits me!")

THE ARRIVAL   The night before the
     1907   anticipated arrival in

New York, Federico was as restless as all the other passengers and could not sleep a wink. Close to dawn, the ship reduced speed and seemed to be merely floating in the faint light of the Morning Star. Then, all of a sudden, through the gray mist, "Lady Liberty," with her uplifted arm bearing a torch, emerged like a heavenly apparition.

Some men held their children on their shoulders so they could see the welcoming symbol of their new life and its promise of opportunity. Some passengers were weeping out of joy and relief, grateful to know that the perils of the journey were now behind them. Some knelt prayerfully on their knees, making the sign of the cross. Others appeared bewildered by the immense cityscape, a phenomenon which they had never before seen or could ever have imagined. A few were frightened and fainted. Still others, oblivious to any sentiment whatsoever, pushed to gain first exit and board the barges that would take them to Ellis Island, a place of great hope, but also of great sorrow, a place that had already earned the doleful name, "Island of Tears."

Despite the great numbers constantly disembarking, the excitement and confusion, and the noisy babble of tongues, the offices of entry at Ellis Island were nevertheless always prepared to conduct strict and orderly procedures: medical exams, inquiries regarding awaiting friends or relatives, the financial solvency of the arrivals, being among some of the matters of primary importance. By the time of Federico's coming, legislation already had been passed to protect the arrivals from exploitative practices such as the *padrone* or labor-broker system and other harmful schemes.

In most respects, the procedures of entry were considerate and humane, but for some of the newcomers, they seemed strange, bewildering or shocking ways, sometimes causing them embarrassment, even humiliation or shame. Still worse, however, certain unfortunate souls, confronted with official rejection and the heartbreaking prospect of immediate deportation, sometimes chose the most despairing and tragic course as a solution—suicide.

As passengers in cabin or second-class, Federico and his friends did not pass through Ellis Island, but rather were given cursory medical exams on board and then were permitted to enter the country through a specially numbered pier.

Hoping to catch one of the morning trains to Washington, Rinaldo, hurriedly but warmly, gave his *abbraccio* and goodbye to Federico and Francesco. Sometime earlier, he had given them the address of his uncles with whom he planned to stay until he had settled himself in a place of his own.

As anxious as he also was to get to Pennsylvania, Francesco was very concerned about Federico who was supposed to seek out a Mister Strasso, a man living in the Mulberry Street neighborhood in the Lower East Side; he had been recommended as someone who could be helpful in finding good lodging and suitable employment. Francesco was very suspicious of this and feared that Federico might be perceived and victimized as an easy "green horn" target or prey.

Mulberry Street fulfilled its reputation and then some—a clamorous "scene of scenes" teeming with hundreds of people and activities: peddlers with pushcarts and horse-drawn wagons; numerous stores and open markets displaying foodstuffs in barrels and wicker baskets, dry goods and countless other sundries—all surrounded by five and six-story tenement buildings, festooned with laundry hanging on thin ropes or wires, or drying over the railings of tiny balconies. In dim side streets, men were lingering, while nearby in cluttered courtyards, small children were playing or just running here and there, helter-skelter. The hubbub, ear-splitting bustle and din of the main thoroughfare were of a kind Federico had never experienced. For a few moments, both young men stood motionless and totally bewildered.

Sometime shortly thereafter, as they passed through a dreary gray alley, Federico noticed an elderly woman staring from her small open window at a barely visible narrow patch of blue sky. He imagined that she was thinking of some beautiful view that may have been hers back home in Italy. Now, from a short distance away, the cheery, upbeat sounds of a hurdy-gurdy added an ironic, mocking twist to the melancholic scene. For this poor soul and so many others, Federico thought, memory was to be the only escape from a reality, a purgatory, so alien, bleak and cheerless.

At one point, they stopped to make an inquiry, and, in a moment of distraction, Federico put down his small trunk to take a note out of his pocket. Within a flash, the trunk was scooped up by two boys who flew into the crowded street. Realizing what had happened, he and Francesco yelled and began running after them. Fortunately, two policemen nearby overheard the commotion and, in a stroke of good timing, caught the boys without the slightest tussle. As they returned the trunk to the shaken, but relieved Federico, he heard one officer murmur to his partner—"These damn garlic-eating dagoes, they let their kids run all over the place. They should all be sent back to hell where they came from."

Francesco also overheard the scurrilous remark and tried to explain what the word "dago" meant and that these hateful attitudes were not that uncommon. However, for the time being, Federico dismissed it. He just was grateful to have regained his trunk.

Surely, it wasn't the clothes in it that mattered to him. In the center of the trunk, he had carefully placed all his precious treasures—the orrery, the prince's gift; his prayerbook with Rosalia's small picture and the Dianthus flower, now dried, which she had given him at parting; and his copy of Dante's *Divine Comedy*. Had he lost these, he thought, he would have been devastated. Given a choice, he probably would have preferred losing his money instead. That, fortunately, was

57

still safe, both the small amount in his pants pocket and, importantly, the very great deal more he had sewn inside his jacket—a sum exchanged shipside that he hoped could launch a bright future in this new land.

Francesco was actually relieved when they failed to locate Mister Strasso. He confessed his suspicions to Federico and his fear that he might have been taken advantage of. Aware of his friend's present predicament, however, Francesco convinced Federico to go along with him to Pittsburgh, reminding him of the old saying—"God closes one door, but always opens another."

In the next letter Federico sent to Rosalia, he recounted all the details of his arrival and his feelings and emotions at viewing the impressive Statue of Liberty.

He made little mention of Mulberry Street, only that his mission there was to no avail, and hence he chose to go to Pennsylvania with his kind friend.

TO PENNSYLVANIA
1907

After the Mulberry Street ordeal, the trip to Pennsylvania was a breath of fresh air. For Federico, it was much more than that: it was an ever-expanding revelation about America. As the train ran its both straight and winding course through plains and tunnels, over high-trussed bridges, and along precipitous stone ledges, Federico marveled at the neatly partitioned farmlands, the road systems, the efficiency at the intervening stations, the easy and simple cordiality of the personnel and passengers. But most of all, he was taken by the majesty of William Penn's verdant dominion—the seemingly endless, towering and shimmering, green-treed mountains.

Federico remembered he had been told that the coasts of Sicily and southern Italy had once been amply forested, but that rapacious practices of felling for shipbuilding, fuel and other needs, as well as the mindless devastation of warfare, had denuded the beautiful sylvan landscape, resulting in serious problems of land erosion that now plagued his generation.

Pittsburgh was still another story, with the brutal price of early industrialization everywhere—ugly factories and mills with smokestacks spewing soot and poison into the air and the lungs of unsuspecting citizens.

Francesco brought Federico to where he had formerly lodged during his first stay and succeeded in renting comfortable and very reasonable accommodations. After several days passed during which he took Federico to see the sights, he renewed contact with some acquaintances, among them a friendly and gregarious Irishman, also a musician like himself, a man who always was on top of the latest news. In the course of conversation, the chubby musician—somewhat of a gourmand—mentioned that he had recently read in the newspaper that citrus fruits and bananas were going to be transported by rail to many more regions of the state than had been the case in past years. He noted the interesting news article proposed that the processing and marketing of bananas, particularly, was still an undertaking requiring clever and novel entrepreneurship, but that it had proved to be very lucrative.

For some strange reason, this caught Federico's attention and interest. He knew he had to find a niche for himself pretty quickly, especially now in this new setting. Could this be a possibility? Would he be remiss not to explore its potential? More inquiries with Francesco's assistance disclosed that in a nearby growing settlement, a few miles northwest of Pittsburgh, there were promising opportunities to secure warehousing facilities along a commercial train route.

THE BANK   Federico's   foremost
    1907   concern was   to open
a bank account and establish a reliable financial foundation to underwrite his intended venture. With the imagination of a born entrepreneur, he already envisioned sales of bananas to vegetable and fruit peddlers, small grocers, restaurateurs, and perhaps sometime later, to larger entities, such as hotels, schools and hospitals. He knew he would need horses, barns, groomers, wagons, a warehouse and a prominent storefront with modest

office space. Of course, from his years of service to the prince in Sicily, many of these things, although now in an entirely different context, would nevertheless be rather familiar to him.

His visit to a relatively new family-owned bank—accompanied by Francesco who had a much better command of English—proved to be full of real promise. Just by happy coincidence, the president, a Mister Norton, was a man with a predilection for all things Italian. It had been cultivated early in his life by his mother who had studied painting in Italy and had become totally enamored of the culture and people. Right from the start, the banker seemed well disposed to hear Federico's plan or proposal. His cordial greeting and friendly handshake put Federico immediately at ease. It all seemed too good to be true.

When Federico brought his money forward, Mister Norton was visibly taken aback. The sum was considerable, most unusual for such a young immigrant. Naturally, Mister Norton wondered how Federico had acquired it. Federico explained, as best he could with the aid of his friend, that he had been very frugal from as long as he could remember, putting every *soldo* or penny away for a rainy day. He noted that the income he received from the prince he had saved in its entirety, given that his room and board had been provided. He had supplemented this with occasional work as a scribe; and lastly, he had received a very generous sum of money from a fortunate archaeological discovery.

Obviously pleased with a new client with such thrifty habits and genuine ambition to succeed, Mister Norton suggested that the greater share of Federico's deposit be positioned to ensure a constant line of credit for inventory, payroll and other weekly or monthly expenses in the proposed new business. More importantly, Mister Norton also strongly recommended that Federico consider buying some shares in his fledgling institution that was still seeking investors. (This invitation was a stroke of exceptional good luck. His decision to invest a relatively modest amount of his money, at this point, would make it possible for him to broaden his financial interests and enterprises in the years to come, making him and his children richer than he could ever imagine!)

THE FIND   The genial banker's curiosity
   1907   had   been piqued. When financial issues had been satisfactorily addressed, Mister Norton pressed Federico to tell him about the so-called "lucky archaeological find." It would be the first time Francesco heard about it, as well.

Federico said that the discovery took place when he was about nineteen years old. He related that while he was supervising the operation of one of the prince's granaries, some workmen who had been digging a small irrigation channel, ran to him in an agitated state, shouting—*"Signù, veni, veni, 'na cosa bedda, 'na cosa bedda ammu truvati, veni, veni subito!"* ("Come, come, Sir, we have found a beautiful thing, a beautiful thing. Come, come quickly!")

Federico said that he hastened to the spot where the workmen had regrouped. There, still half-buried in the earth, was an exquisite life-size statue of a female figure. He advised them not to dig any further at the moment but to begin brushing the object lightly. When they re-entered the cavity and began, they felt something close by. Removing more earth with their bare hands, they uncovered a second, slightly smaller figure, again a female subject. Federico then told the men to cover both figures with cloths or leaves, whatever they could find, while he went quickly to inform the prince.

When Prince Bronte came, he instructed the men to raise the figures very carefully. When they had done so, Federico could see that the prince was awe-struck, with tears in his eyes. He then asked, "Do you know the ancient deities these beautiful marble figures represent? This large one is the Greek goddess, Demeter. The Romans called her Ceres. She is the goddess of agriculture. Look, see the corn depicted on her headdress and the sheaf of long grain she is holding? The smaller figure clutching a tiny bouquet is her daughter, Proserpina. According to the story or belief, she was carried away and detained, during the wintertime, as the consort of the god of the underworld, Pluto. In the spring and for the duration of the other fair seasons, she would be returned to her grieving mother who missed her so. These images symbolize the seasonal patterns of scarcity in winter, Proserpina's period of capture, and of abundance in spring, summer and fall, her time of release or liberation into the company of her now jubilant parent."

"It is perhaps not unusual that these figures are here. We are just southeast of the flowery plains of Enna where the episode of Proserpina's abduction, while she was gathering blooms, was believed to have taken place. It was considered a sacred site and it is where, many centuries ago, our Greek forebears dedicated a shrine to her and her mother's memory."

Federico could see that the workmen, humble and simple as they might have been, were nevertheless very moved by this account. They seemed especially touched by the prince's sympathetic description of the disconsolate mother goddess, who, having lit her torch on Mount Etna, went frantically searching every bedimmed and dark place of the island, hoping to rescue her child from such a grim and dolorous fate. Perhaps they had daughters of their own and could identify with her plight.

Federico admitted that he could hardly hold back his own emotions. He sensed that such stories or myths held essential truths about the human condition and felt that he had been favored, in some mysterious way, to have been part of this unusual discovery.

The prince then warned them not to tell anyone about this, especially any government authorities. If these officials were corrupt, he noted, they would confiscate the statues and sell them off for their own personal gain.

Sometime after, when the statues had been cleaned, the prince had them installed in special niches he had prepared in the rotunda entry of his palace. He also commissioned a local artist to paint an inscription directly above the niches, combining the words of Theocritus, the Sicilian creator of the idyll, and Shelley, the English lyric poet, to read:

"Demeter, rich in fruit and rich in grain,
breathe Thine influence, most divine,
upon Thine own child, Proserpine"

The prince intended to keep them close to where they had been found. In order to ensure that they would not fall someday into private hands at some distant place, but rather that the people of Sicily and the larger world beyond would be able to see and cherish them, he listed them in the codicil attached to his will, with the stipulation that they be donated, at his death, to the principal archaeological museum at Palermo.

(Only later did Federico learn that the prince had refrained from disclosing to him and the workmen the belief that if an image of this mother-earth goddess were to be moved very far away, the land she had presided over would go barren.

Was it conceivable that the prince, a modern, rational man, may secretly have subscribed to this?)

Federico then said there was still more to tell regarding this story. Several weeks after the statues had been cleaned (miraculously, they were intact with no breakage or other damage) and installed in the palace, the prince called him and the three workmen to the business office in the palace service quarters where accounts were kept and salaries dispensed on appointed days.

The prince, being an astute but also a fair man, praised the workmen for their honesty in making the wonderful discovery known to him. He admitted that they could have chosen to conceal the statues and, although it could have proven dangerous or risky, attempted to sell them secretly. (As a well-versed classicist, no doubt he was very familiar with the story of the avaricious peasant who discovered the armless Venus on the Aegean island of Melos a long time before.)

Having said that, to the surprise of all, the prince then gave the workmen each an equal sum of money, enough to buy a modest parcel of land on which to grow whatever they needed or desired for themselves and their families. As he dismissed them, he asked Federico to remain and, in turn, gave him a very large sum of money which he said he could choose to save or use in whatever way he saw fit. He then brought him to the chief accountant, whom Federico, of course, already knew, and requested that he be trained in basic bookkeeping. (This new proficiency added to Federico's other duties and augmented his income appreciably before his departure for America. It would also serve him well later in his own businesses.)

Federico acknowledged to Mister Norton and his friend, Francesco, that he was often haunted by this extraordinary experience. He wondered many times over who had created these works of art, who had put them in some special place of honor to be admired, perhaps adored, and what could possibly have led to their mysterious burial in the earth. Had they been hidden long ago to prevent them from becoming the spoils of some war or conflict, and then forgotten? Were they disapproved as objects of pagan veneration and banished by the early church?

Although these treasures of a smiling antique Sicilian world had been sleeping for centuries, when they returned to the light of day, they awakened something familiar and deeply resonant in Federico, heightening and enriching his perspective on life. Recalling the emotions and rapture they all shared at the time—he, the prince and the humble workmen—he wondered, as well, what it was in his people's historical experience or collective memory that made the Sicilian soul so susceptible to "the beautiful" and enthralled by tales and visions of mythic glory.

BANANAS AND THE SPIDER 1908

Remarkably, within four or five months, Federico had almost all aspects of his business operational. Until the college year was in full session, and even after, his good friend, Francesco, made several trips, back and forth from Pittsburgh, to help him get established.

While addressing such legal matters as the publishing of a business name, health standard requirements and other regulations and permits, Federico also succeeded in purchasing horses, wagons, and a barn with smith and groomer services. Very much to his liking, he found an old, but serviceable two-storey building on the periphery of the downtown area, with the most necessary feature of all—direct rail line access.

The main level of the building had enough space for Federico to set up rooms toward the rear for the processing and curing of the bananas, as well as a very large area in the front for a small office and his wholesale and retail food provision market which would be tendering imported products such as olive oil, pastas, preserved meats, cheeses, candies, and many other non-perishable Italian staples.

In his free time, mostly in the evening, he took saw, hammer and nail in hand and divided the greater part of the equally large second floor area into several rooms, including a functioning kitchen, bath and bedroom where he could live, rather spartanly at first, but more comfortably when Rosalia would come.

Over the wide window and door of the building, streetside, he proudly hung a large sign, in the Sicilian pennant colors of deep red and yellow, which read: "F. D'Argenti Company, Banana and Imported Foods Provisioner. "

The arrival of the first carload of bananas was an unforgettable event for Federico and some of his new employees— two Irishmen, brothers Sean and Kevin Cleary; a Pole, Stanley Jankowiak; and three Italians, Nino Montesano and Ciro Bruni from Calabria and Calogero Ranieri from Sicily. (These men would remain loyal to Federico until their retirements; where practical and appropriate, he would move them or their educated children into more important positions within his later diverse enterprises).

It was a dark, chilly morning at four-thirty—one like thousands more to come—when the screeching boxcar was positioned next to the giant metal door which opened on to a wide concrete ramp and loading dock. Federico and his men were amazed at the sight of the bananas that had survived such a long trip from the ship in Louisiana. The vivid green bunches were still attached to their long tree stems hanging from large, strong hooks attached to the boxcar ceiling. It was a novel task. The men removed them carefully, one by one—they were awkward and heavy—and brought them into the warehouse rooms where they would again be suspended from hooks.

(After some trial and error, the ripening and processing procedures would work out to be about seventy-two hours, concluding with bunches being cut, weighed and placed into paper-lined boxes for delivery. Very early on, Federico sophisticated the operation for ripening and coloring the fruit by fitting the storerooms with metal walls and ceilings equipped with gas-controlled lines. Many years later, when air conditioning became available at reasonable cost, he would have it installed in the entire building.)

The Central American shipping company had alerted Federico to exercise caution when unloading because occasionally a snake or insect, possibly poisonous and dangerous, might survive the trip. Federico had hardly begun to utter a warning to that effect to his men when suddenly a huge, hairy black spider dropped to the railroad car floor and attempted to conceal itself under some molding. Two of the workmen screamed. Kevin jumped forward fearlessly and tried to put an inverted open tin can over the spot where the spider had hidden. In a booming voice, Stanley yelled "Kevin, let the spider go, let it jump down on the rail, if you can. Spiders can be signs of luck, the larger their size, the greater the luck." The others caught their breath and looked at each other with a mixture of disbelief and a mild case of the jitters.

To Federico's way of thinking, this unloading was an important inaugural event and so, in advance, he planned a little celebration for his workers. After the car had been completely emptied and the bananas put in place, he had the local baker deliver some fresh, man-sized pastries. To complement these sugary treats, he provided some very strong coffee capped with a half-jigger of homemade liqueur, an aromatic tonic which succeeded in bracing the tired men and settling their jangled nerves. During this moment of well-deserved repose, Sean lifted his cup, toasted the spider, and in a corncrake voice, sang a little Irish ditty: "While we live, let's live in clover, for when we're dead, we're dead all over!"

For many years thereafter, on the anniversary date of this event, Federico and his employees, old and new, would enjoy the sharing of pastries and a little spiked coffee. It was an occasion to reminisce about the early times and debate about the advances and changes in technology for preparing and delivering their product.

At the outset, Federico's sales and distribution, with teams of horses and wagons, operated modestly within a working radius of about ten to twenty miles. After a short while, it advanced to thirty; and later, with motorized truck transport, it exceeded fifty miles, covering several small urban and rural areas, and numbering hundreds of retail grocery establishments, restaurants, hospitals and hotels, and eventually, university campus facilities. Within several decades, all this would be dwarfed by an astonishingly sophisticated mega-scale food distribution company operating on a national scale.

Although the year 1907 was probably one of the most inauspicious times to establish a new business in America, Federico was convinced, from the start, that he had a unique and desirable product, and more importantly, he was determined to succeed no matter what obstacles—*"Volontá!"* "Will!"

Undeniably, Federico was first and foremost a serious business man, but now and then, his more sentimental, even fanciful side, manifested itself. For years, he kept an old wagon in a dusty corner of the warehouse as a hallowed memento or relic of these early times, especially as a reminder of the very first day and the scary but good omen of the spider.

MARRIAGE   At the close of his
    1910   last letter to Rosalia,
Federico wrote—"As you cross the vast
ocean, *cara*, whenever you look at the
wide open sky, picture inscribed there—
'Federico loves Rosalia! Come quickly!'"

    Almost three years had passed
since Federico pledged his love to Rosalia
and promised he would call for her to
come to America. Now that his business
affairs were faring well, he felt confident
that he could support a wife and family
with some measure of comfort. He had
modestly furnished the apartment above
the store and warehouse, hoping that

Rosalia would like it and give it the feminine touch that makes an ordinary place a home.

It was only natural that Rosalia looked to her new life in a strange land with some degree of trepidation. She had never set foot very far beyond the confines of the convent, her home for almost sixteen years. Usually it was just an excursion with the sisters to some other religious house or public event in the local area or a not-too-distant town. She had never seen a very large city other than grand Siracusa, and that just once. Only in her formal studies with the Ursulines— in history, geography and music—had she travelled, in her mind's eye, to distant places and cultures.

When it was certain that Rosalia would be leaving in a matter of a few weeks, the sisters rushed to complete the many things they had been making, over several months, for her *corredo* or trousseau. This was a custom still observed in late nineteenth and early twentieth century Sicily. A young woman from a good, respectable family was expected to bring such to the marriage union. It could include money, jewelry and property, but most of the time it was just simple material things for establishing a new home. In a visible and tangible way, it represented the girl's social standing, reflected in the quantity and quality of items—beautiful handmade bed linens, tablecloths, dresses, cloaks and shawls, shoes, delicate undergarments, and so forth. Unstated, the *corredo* was a kind of guarantee or insurance for maintaining a certain standard of living for a young woman in her new social position, as a wife and eventually, also a mother.

While the sisters busied themselves and Rosalia with these pleasant tasks, Mother Maria Antonietta, the Superior, was preoccupied with two other very important matters: arrangement of Rosalia's marriage by proxy and finding suitable companions for her ocean voyage. In some instances, women did travel alone, but Mother Antonietta would never contemplate this even as a remote possibility for her charge, the little girl she had raised almost like a daughter. Her first few efforts failed, but finally she found a couple returning to America who would make pleasant and respectable company for Rosalia. Although their destination was their home in upstate New York, they promised that they would not proceed with their own plans until Rosalia was properly met by Federico and they were sure she was safely on her way to her new home in Pennsylvania.

Arrangements for the proxy marriage were somewhat simple. Mother Antonietta requested the son of one of the convent's benefactors to stand in for the brief ceremony at the office of the *sindaco* or mayor. This civil process, conferring documented legal marital status on Rosalia as "Mrs. Federico D'Argenti," would make her entry into America relatively routine.

The day of Rosalia's departure from the convent was one of both joy and sadness. The sisters gathered around her tearfully, holding her hands and hugging her. Although she was excited and happy beyond measure, Rosalia had all she could do from breaking down. Even Mother Antonietta, always a picture of composure no matter what the situation, was in an emotional state her younger spiritual charges had never witnessed. Wiping away a tear and with her voice quavering, she said – "Dearest child, Rosalia, I must confess I fear for you – the long ocean crossing, the unknowns of your life in a new country. Remember that I and the sisters will always pray for you and be here if ever you need us." Then she moved to a table nearby and presented Rosalia with a lovely ivory prayerbook and said – "Carry this, dear child, at your wedding ceremony in your new land, and whenever you pray from it, think of me and how much I and the sisters have loved you."

The sisters all began to cry again. Sister Agnes then approached Rosalia with a long white box. She urged Rosalia to open it quickly. There, folded in delicate blue tissue, was an exquisite christening gown she had made. Touching the long lace at its bottom, entwined with pink and blue ribbon, sister said – "Rosalia, my little companion and sweetest friend, this is for your children. May they have my blessing when they enter into the grace of Holy Mother Church." And she kissed Rosalia goodbye and rushed out of the room.

Federico had taken a very small vessel from Messina to Naples in order to board a large ship for the ocean voyage. This was no longer possible. A great earthquake in 1908, two years before Rosalia's departure, had destroyed the city of Messina, with many, many, thousands perishing. At the same time, a tidal wave of tremendous force brought great destruction across the strait to parts of Calabria as well. Consequently, Rosalia and her travelling companions, Giuseppe and Concetta Dispenza, now had to journey a much greater distance to Palermo where they then would board a small launch to the waiting steamship that would take them to America.

Federico was accompanied to New York by his friend, Francesco, and

Elena, his wife of just a few months. The plan was for Rosalia to stay with them in Pittsburgh until the wedding a week or so later. They arrived a bit late to the pier after some unforeseen delays in the city.

When Federico saw Rosalia descending to the pier, accompanied by her chaperons, he was awe-struck. He remembered a demure girl who was often attired in just a simple dress. Now she appeared like a vision to him. She had the mien of a mature, polished young woman. His heartbeat quickened.

Rosalia was wearing a lavender-colored, fitted two-piece crepe traveling suit. Its revers, edges and skirt-bottom were trimmed in aubergine velvet; the buttons of the bodice and those down one side of the skirt, as well as on the elaborately embroidered sleeve cuffs, were of the same dark shade. Her dainty, heeled shoes—barely visible under her long skirt—were also covered in matching velvet. Rosalia's hair was fashioned in the popular "Gibson Girl" style, with a plain tortoise-shell comb at the back. A tiny black veil attached to a small lavender hat, and a single curl or ringlet coming down each side of her face, framed her beautiful and delicate features. Her only jewelry was a leaf-shaped gold pin centered high on the neck of her écru-colored lace blouse, and small, also leaf-shaped, gold earrings, each set with a single tiny amethyst stone at the center. Her patterned gloves and the small, tightly pleated silk clutch she held were of a light lavender color.

Federico moved quickly toward her. He embraced her, giving her a kiss on her cheek which she, briefly looking into his eyes, eyes that appeared adoring and misty, ardently returned. After warm but brief introductions, the Dispenzas departed and the young foursome hurried to claim Rosalia's trunk. An hour or so later, after taking a little something to eat at a nearby restaurant and finding delight in Rosalia's excitement and fascination with the sights and pace of the city, they boarded a train headed for Pittsburgh.

Federico planned a simple wedding. The service was scheduled for one o'clock in the afternoon of September 4th, the day that coincided with Rosalia's *onomastico*, the feastday of her patron saint, Saint Rosalia, a greatly revered figure in Sicilian, particularly Palermitan, religious tradition.

The setting was idyllic: a small, white woodframe chapel, set on a low hill dotted with wildflowers and surrounded by tall pine trees. It was in an area not far from the city. Federico had discovered it, just by chance, one Sunday afternoon while he was hiking. Curious, he had made inquiries and learned that the little structure had been abandoned with no one ever claiming ownership. All that was known about it was that some itinerant preachers had used it at one time to hold simple services on their revival route.

Sometime before Rosalia's expected late August arrival, Federico and some of his employees had cleaned it—removing the accumulation of decades of dried leaves and cobwebs—and then given it a fresh coat of paint wherever it seemed needed. They also set up chairs (which they had hauled on one of the banana wagons) to be used first for the indoor service and afterward for the outdoor reception.

By virtue of her Italian proxy, Rosalia was already legally Federico's wife. However, respecting her religious upbringing and given his own reverential attitude toward things sacred, Federico asked a young priest from his parish church to come and officiate for the exchange of their vows and to bless their union.

On the special day, Rosalia wore an ankle-length deep cream-colored dress she had brought with her from Sicily, and matching shoes which, with Elena's help, she had found and purchased in Pittsburgh. A veil, attached to a delicate headpiece, and tiny gold earrings, completed her ensemble. She carried a small nosegay of miniature roses, attached with ribbons to the prayerbook Mother Antonietta had given her on the day she departed from the convent.

Federico wore a simple dark suit, a white shirt with a stiff high collar and a white tie pierced with a pin set with a very small ruby.

Their rings were of simple unadorned gold.

Francesco and Elena stood as the witnesses and Federico's employees, their spouses or friends, and one or two of his new business associates and their spouses, made up the guests.

On the grassy area in front of the chapel, Federico had arranged tables with cloths on which little cakes, cookies and other desserts, sugar-coated almonds, Marsala and other sweet wines were served. Francesco brought two of his students from the college to provide music: a violinist for the couple's entry to and from the chapel, and an accordionist for the reception outdoors.

After a brief but touching service in which the priest addressed the couple and blessed the rings as they professed their love and commitment, the reception began. Francesco raised his glass and reminisced about how he met Federico, and all their many experiences. Then he gave a brief toast, saying:

> "May your joys be as deep as the ocean,
> And your misfortunes as light as
> its foam."

As the music began, one of Federico's employees said, "Aren't you going to dance with your bride, Mister D'Argenti?" Federico needed little encouragement. He took Rosalia by the hand, placed his arm around her tiny waist and began to dance. Fittingly, it was a Neapolitan love song, Di Capua's moving "Serenade of the Roses." Before the end of the third measure, the spouses of the Italian employees came forward. Swaying with the music, they began to wrap long, thin, multi-colored paper streamers around the dancing couple. All present then joined in the dancing. With Francesco's lead mimicking the motions of a conductor, they began chanting in unison, "Best wishes and good luck to Federico and his bride, his beautiful rose from Sicily."

As the reception came to a close under a shower of rice and confetti, Federico kissed his bride lightly on the lips. She blushed. He too. It was their first, ever.

A NEW LIFE TOGETHER 1910   Federico somehow managed to get a few orange leaves which, in keeping with an old Sicilian nuptial tradition, he placed on the floor at the entrance to the apartment. As he lifted Rosalia in his arms and crossed the threshold, he stepped on the leaves and he kissed her, saying, "Welcome home, my love, I hope this is to your liking, as simple and humble as it is."

Rosalia ran hastily from room to room, exclaiming how airy and pretty the apartment was. True, it was by no means luxurious—she hadn't expected that—but the fact that he had prepared it for her was reason enough, she thought, to let him know how pleased she was. "To think, Federico," she said, "all my life I have been in the company and care of the sisters, I never really had to worry or even think about taking care of myself—and here you have been fending for yourself all alone, day by day, while working hard at your business, as well, all just for me, for us. I want so much to be your helpmate. I love you Federico, and I promise I will do all I can to make you happy. I know I need to learn many new things, but you will help me, won't you, Federico?" Hugging and pressing her close, he responded, "Of course, dearest, we are one now."

The sky was quickly turning to rose and amethyst. Their special day was coming to its close. Long anticipated but now behind them—the setting, the ceremony, the friends and felicitations, the music, dancing and laughter—were to be the things of which precious memories are made. Suddenly, a rush of yearning fell upon them both. Holding one another at the waist, they moved, trancelike, into the bedroom where their souls and bodies merged, surrendering to a night of sweet ecstasy, to feelings, sighs and passion hereto unknown to them.

The first months were times for adjustment to one another, the give-and-take of shared living, getting to know one another's habits, likes and dislikes, and little idiosyncrasies. Federico gradually and gently introduced Rosalia to some of his routine, while at the same time encouraging her English and creating little tasks, other than the normal household concerns, that would assist him and give her a sense of belonging and helping.

Much like her husband, Rosalia was a quick study and was soon capable of handling a share of the front store retail activity, as well as some of the minor bookkeeping and other office details. This freed Federico to address many of the other new interests that were demanding his time and close attention. (The fact that they were both literate gave them a very great advantage over other immigrants who had not had sufficient or any schooling whatsoever.)

In a short while, as Federico had anticipated, Rosalia added beautiful little things—curtains and pillows, pictures, plants, bibelots and other adornments— giving their apartment a homey and welcoming feeling.

Word had spread quickly that Federico had taken a wife and a very beautiful one at that. Some customers, men and women too, curious to see for themselves, made any excuse—even to buy something they didn't really need—in order to get a glimpse of her.

One day, a neatly dressed but manifestly inebriated man approached the front counter. Upon seeing Rosalia, he pushed his way toward Federico who had his back to the room. The man scoffed in a shrill voice, "How the hell did you ever get such a beautiful broad? Is she for sale too?" Federico began to turn to face him, saying – "How dare you brazen…"—but before he could finish the sentence, the man jumped him. Infuriated, Federico swiftly landed a rabbit punch on the man's neck. Stunned, he fell to the floor. Some customers quickly surrounded him, making sure he didn't take off.

Arriving within minutes, the neighborhood patrolman assured Federico – "Don't worry, Mister D'Argenti – it was self-defense. He's too drunk to have been hurt. I'll see that he stays in the slammer until he's sober. Do you want to press charges?" "No," said Federico, rushing to Rosalia who was still shaking and sobbing in a far corner of the room. Federico had all he could do to calm her and convince her that this was just a terrible fluke, something that would never happen again.

By the next year's close, Federico and Rosalia would have their first child, a daughter, Giulietta; three years later, it would be a son, Fabrizio, whom Federico would name after his benefactor, Prince Fabrizio Bronte. Rosalia embraced the joys and tasks of young motherhood while still continuing to help Federico as she had at the beginning. It involved quite a delicate balancing act between the apartment with the little ones and the business below.

THE CHILDREN   Home   life   with
1911, 1914   Rosalia   and   the
children gave Federico sanctuary, a haven
where he could forget his driven business
cares.   Watching his children grow and
sharing in their new experiences were
sweet, precious moments that anchored
and refreshed him and gave him a happy
heart.

From the start, Giulietta, their
first-born, was a delicate and sensitive
child who brought her parents joy in great
measure.   Federico welcomed his dainty
little cherub's antics and her delight and
glee in the smallest things—a flower, a
ragdoll's tea party, dancing to a simple
melody her mother would play on the old
upright piano.

One day when he took her to a
park when she was no more than three
or four years old, she saw a butterfly for
the first time.   Excited, she ran to him,
exclaiming, "Come, papá, come see a

'birdflower'!" Federico marveled at the child's reasoning; she knew "flower" and "bird" and had spontaneously created a touching expressive figure. It made Federico muse, "When humankind was young, did language begin like this, in childlike awe and poetry?"

From the earliest, Giulietta exhibited a devout, religious spirit. It would be she who would remind everyone that it was time to say the family rosary either in the morning or in the early evening right after dinner.

Giulietta was a good student at the private school she attended in her early teen years. It was here that she became fondly attached to the nuns, her teachers, whom she admired a great deal. Hence, it was no surprise when she told her parents that she wished to enter the religious life. At the age of nineteen, she began her novitiate; five years later, she would profess her final vows in the community of the Missionary Sisters of the Sacred Heart, an order founded in 1880 by Mother Frances Cabrini who, on papal request, had come to America to establish schools, hospitals and orphanages for the care of Italian immigrants.

Giulietta became very involved in the care of orphans, a cause which was close to her parents' hearts, given their own personal histories. As his fortune grew, Federico gave generously to Giulietta's religious community and its charitable undertakings. One of his final gifts would be a perpetual trust for Giulietta's special program for disabled orphan children.

Despite the constraints and demands of her religious calling, over the years Giulietta would keep constant contact with her parents and her brother whom she loved very much.

From the beginning, their son Fabrizio—named after the prince—was also a good child, never unmanageable or disobedient. All his early years, spent in the city center, were rather ordinary and devoid of any rebellion or angst. However, with the family's eventual move to the wealthy hill district and the onset of puberty, Fabrizio's personality would begin to change.

Despite Federico's earnest attachment to many aspects of the American way of life, a moderate case of cultural and generational conflict would begin to manifest itself between father and son. In some ways, this was both predictable and inevitable, a common phenomenon in the process of assimilation.

In the new suburban environment, Fabrizio experienced subtle expressions of prejudice that were particularly hurtful. This wasn't easy to recognize because, outwardly at least, he was fully involved in school and extracurricular activities, including many hours spent in sports, an activity his father, Federico, found rather difficult to understand. "All this ball playing," Fabrizio would often hear, "Where is it going to get you? Better you practice the piano! It's something that will enrich you for a lifetime."

Fabrizio chose to turn somewhat of a deaf ear. Whatever it would take, he was absolutely determined to "fit in" and to be accepted as "American." He became insistent that he be called "Fab", attempting to conceal the identity of his given Italian name. Later, he preferred being called "Stephen" or "Steve", the middle name he had chosen at his confirmation. He began signing his name as "F. Stephen D'Argenti."

One day, when he rather breezily and boldly proposed to his father that they change their last name to "Silver" (*argento* meaning silver in Italian), Federico's incredulous, frosty stare turned into an angry glare and outburst –

"Enough! That's the last straw! Don't you go on proposing any more such nonsense! What kind of a man do you want to be? One who hides in the shadows? You should be proud of your heritage. You'll probably never hear it in school, but just remember that Italians have made many contributions to this great country, way before and after Washington's time! And it's up to young people like you to uphold their legacy and build on it."

It seemed strange, if not somewhat out-of-character, that Federico didn't exhibit compassion or empathy for his son's predicament. Was it because he had experienced more blatant, "in-your-face" bigotry of a much uglier variety? Or did he wish that his son would learn to cope with hardship or adversity with a manly fortitude? Rosalia, however, understood her son's pain and dilemma—feeling caught in an ambiguous middle, so to speak—and she treated the sensitive subject with her characteristic calm and gentleness, while always assuring him of his father's abiding love.

In the long run, this adolescent turmoil turned out to be only a phase in growing up and facing life's realities and challenges. After attending university and earning a graduate degree in business management, Fabrizio would engage, with talent and energy, in his father's many-faceted enterprises and financial interests. A several-year stint in military service, as an enlisted navy man, would change some of his attitudes but not, unfortunately, his fundamental temperament.

Giulietta had inherited, in large measure, the serene nature of their mother; however, as he entered middle adulthood, Fabrizio began to suffer from a malaise, as if he were burdened with a discontent or sorrow, some troubling remnant from another time or past. Gratefully, however, when he was distressed or inclined to be irritable, his remedy at home was to sit and play the piano for an hour or two. He had exhibited a special gift for this instrument from the very first lessons he received at his mother's knee, when just a little fellow of four or five. Several years of study with excellent teachers eventually brought him to an impressive level of ability and accomplishment.

Despite his melancholy and, at times, highly sensitive and cantankerous behavior, Fabrizio was, at the core, a good, kind-hearted and well-meaning individual.

A NEED, Federico and A CHALLENGE Rosalia were just 1917 children when they first met at the May religious celebration in Noto. Federico would readily admit that he had been taken first by Rosalia's beauty, but even at that young age, there were intangible attributes that especially attracted him—her intelligence, her uncommon grace of person and her quiet strength. She was one of those rare individuals who looked upon life, in all its aspects, both good and bad, with an innate serenity, a kind of natural equanimity, if you will.

Rosalia seemed truly wise beyond her years. Was it due, in part, to the tragic loss of her mother while still an infant or was it the years in the company of the good sisters? Or was it both? Possessed of an unusual capacity for understanding the feelings of others, she responded to even the most difficult persons and situations with forbearance and kindness. Numerous times she told Federico that she preferred to ignore the unpleasant things in others and to affirm the positive. When she imputed the good, she said, almost always good things followed. Her preference, she acknowledged, was captured in the old saying that "commendation is always better than reproof." Even if she were disappointed with some people, she often reserved judgment and gave the benefit of the doubt. She realized, of course, that many may have thought her foolish or naive, but she didn't mind.

For those in need, in a cause close to home or a distant foreign relief effort, she wasn't averse to some type of impersonal help, be it the writing of a check or an anonymous donation; however, she really preferred one-to-one personal charity.

Federico, on the other hand, while always suave and a paragon of courtesy, responded instinctively to others, and even though his quick judgments were often on target, so to speak, there was much he admired and loved about Rosalia's more tender and benign outlook and behavior. In so many ways, she never failed to be his anchor and his inspiration. Although she never made any unreasonable demands on him, whenever she expressed an idea or wish, he was always ready to listen and to fulfill her desire. His boundless love for her would court no other response. She was, simply and totally, the idol of his heart.

Days led to months and the months to the stretch of several years. Life had become routine and comfortable, in many ways perhaps too predictable. Federico's diverse businesses were expanding and thriving, but he began to sense a certain vague restlessness at home. It wasn't a palpable, overt thing, but something that would be perceptible, nevertheless, to a caring spouse.

One day, he asked Rosalia – "Is something troubling you darling? There are times I sense you are preoccupied." Glancing away and hesitating, Rosalia responded softly, "Perhaps." "Perhaps what?" Federico persisted. Again, a small silence. Then she said –

"I couldn't ask for more, Federico. I have you, our beautiful children. We work very hard, we're aiming for a more comfortable future, a beautiful new home, yet ..."

She seemed reluctant to continue. Then she sweetly repined, "I feel something is missing, like I should be doing something for others – perhaps it's my upbringing with the sisters who were always looking for ways to do good." With a puzzled look and seeming to object, Federico responded –

"But *amore*, I'm somewhat baffled. At present, you are doing so much. As they say, you already have a full plate!"

"I know, Federico, but I still feel that I should be helping others. I've noticed how many poor people are moving into the city here, right in our very neighborhood. The men have their work, however unpleasant it may often be, but many of the women seem to be lost in such strange and unfamiliar surroundings and circumstances. In some ways, I can certainly identify with them. Perhaps they would benefit just from the company of other women and know they can rely on some understanding and support.

Federico understood what she was saying; he himself had been witnessing the very things Rosalia had observed. Placing his hand gently on her shoulder, he said with a reassuring smile, "Let's put our heads together, dearest, I'm sure we can do something. Yes, it's very true, we have been working hard; we are prospering. But you are right, we should think of others and their needs as well. You've reminded me of one of my old teachers who often used to quote an ancient poet's prescription for a truly fulfilling life. It went something like this: 'If you are prosperous but not kind, you invite calamity, but if you are both prosperous and kind, you stand at the happy top of the world.'"

During the next few weeks, Federico sought out the ideas of two newcomers from Italy, both professionals, one a pharmacist, the other, a lawyer. Although they were busy attempting to establish themselves, they were willing to join Federico, convinced of his and Rosalia's objectives. After a few discussions, they decided to establish a benevolent or mutual aid society, but they needed a meeting place or headquarters to get it underway. Within a short time, through his connections, Federico was able to lease an empty store-front building in the downtown area, in a location easily accessed by foot or short tram ride.

The front part of the building had ample space for a small office and a large meeting room. In the rooms to the back, Rosalia would be able to conduct afternoon and early evening classes for the women.

Within a very short time and with her natural creative aplomb, Rosalia developed novel programs devoted to shopping, cooking, health and child care, and sewing, the latter including lace-making and embroidery, two skills she had been taught by the Ursulines. For the younger set, she also held after-school classes in music and in drawing, the latter another interest and talent that had been cultivated by the sisters at the convent in Noto.

Through contacts at the business, Rosalia and Federico secured the aid of some women in the larger community who were disposed to teach English and the rudiments of reading and writing. Federico's new friend and associate, the attorney, designed classes in civics and citizenship for both men and women.

After one of Rosalia's sessions, a woman approached her and said, "Signora D'Argenti, my daughter came with me the other afternoon. When we returned home, she said to me, 'Isn't Misses D'Argenti a beautiful and nice lady? I want to be like her when I grow up.'" Blushing, Rosalia thanked the woman. In her heart, she had a good feeling, trusting that Mother Antonietta would be especially pleased with her efforts. She recalled that when she was a child at the convent, the loving nun often drew upon examples from the lives of the saints to encourage her to find little ways of being helpful and doing good for others.

As she prepared to return home,

Rosalia said a little prayer, silently—
"Sweet Jesus, guide me and Federico
in this venture, for the welfare of these
people in need and for your honor and
glory."

Although strictly "home-grown,"
so to speak, these efforts resembled
the programs of the settlement house
movement introduced by Jane Addams at
Hull House in Chicago some years before.
In time, the mutual aid society would be
reconstituted as an active lodge of the
national organization of The Order of
the Sons of Italy, founded earlier in 1905
by the Sicilian physician, Dr. Vincenzo
Sellaro.

Federico and Rosalia would
continue with these programs long after
their move from the center city.   Of
course, as the need for certain services

or programs diminished, they were quickly replaced by new goals, such as the provision of scholarships for Italian and other succeeding immigrant children. Still other grander philanthropic causes, on a community level and far beyond, would be eventually addressed by a well-endowed D'Argenti family foundation, an entity benefitting from Federico's business acumen and Rosalia's gifts of discernment, empathy and special human touch.

Part Three
1925 - 1929

THE MANSION   It was hard to believe

     1925   that almost fifteen
years had passed since Federico and
Rosalia had begun their married life in
the apartment above the business. Up to
the present, it hadn't been easy raising
the children, Fabrizio, ten, and Giulietta,
going on fourteen, in such an environment.
There had been virtually no yard to play
in, only a little enclosed park fronting
the protestant church a few yards away
from their store. Besides the old electric
trolley, the growing auto and truck traffic
presented new unfamiliar danger, so that
even sidewalk play was now totally out of
the question.

The city was getting very congested and noisy and they wanted, more than ever, to provide the children with safe, healthy and serene surroundings, and more importantly, the chance to have friends their age nearby. For themselves, they desired land to grow flowers, herbs and vegetables, and (Federico's special interest) to cultivate select varieties of fruit trees. Also, like many others, they subscribed to "The American Dream" and desired a large and elegant home, a fitting emblem which would represent the harvest of their years of hard work and sacrifices and reflect the level of their substantial financial success.

Every free moment at his disposal—and there were not many he could set aside—Federico would drive his new black "Runabout" through the areas surrounding the city, finally finding and falling in love with a large acreage fronting on a recently platted wide boulevard in the hill district. At some distance from the center of the city and reached by only one serpentine, somewhat hazardous road, it was, nevertheless, regarded as a choice location. Years before, some of the early settlers or founding families had built modest summer cottages there, but now, more and more, it was considered the most desirable residential area by aspiring, upwardly mobile professional and business people. Upon viewing it, Rosalia agreed that it would be the perfect setting for a splendid home.

In his mind, Federico had often recalled the opulence and splendor of the prince's palace. He neither could replicate the palace, nor in any way did he wish to. However, he was certain he wanted a stately home, appointed with whatever American-style amenities and comforts he could now afford.

When he called upon a leading Pittsburgh architect, he told him – "I want

something rather grand but American."
Somewhat amused, the architect
responded quickly, "Why not something
American with Italian inspiration?"
Federico retorted, "Do you mean what
I've seen so far called 'Italianate'? Hasn't
it been around for a while? I'm not sure
I want that!" "No," the architect replied,
"I'm thinking Georgian. It's classic and
forever, and your countryman, Palladio,
you may or may not know, is the original
artistic influence and inspiration."

Federico queried, "Can you do it
in brick?" "Sir, not only brick, but we'll
do the roof in slate and all the gutters
and special fittings in copper as well."
Federico thought for a while, then said
– "You haven't said how much it will
cost, but if you design some beautiful
plans that my wife will approve, and
promise me you'll personally supervise
the construction, it's a deal." "Mister
D'Argenti, I'm happy and ready to do it

if you're ready to pay for it!" "Let's get it done," concluded Federico.

From the first turn of soil to the very last nail, Federico and Rosalia watched the construction of their dream home. The final creation was an imposing three-storey structure entirely of a deep red brick. It had a striking elevation. The grand central entrance was surmounted by a large Palladian window which would admit light into the hall and staircase of the interior.

The front roof was adorned with a modillioned cornice, three pedimented dormers and an elegant wood balustrade atop its upper slate slope. On one side of the house, a large conservatory jutted out; on the other, a delicately columned *porte cochere*, with a sunroom above.

Sited deep into the acreage, the house was approached through a gated circular driveway composed of crushed stone. A huge detached garage, with an apartment above, was at the back of the property, concealed behind a long row of tall evergreen trees.

The ground floor was styled, in customary Georgian fashion, with a central corridor, front to back, a huge entry hall with a grand staircase leading to the second level, and all the remaining rooms symmetrically arranged, left and right. These included a large livingroom with a fireplace, a library also with a fireplace, the two sunrooms, a kitchen, powderoom, and a ballroom, the most elaborate area in all the house. This very large chamber had a high vaulted ceiling, a Murano glass chandelier (Federico was able to order from Venice), and *grisaille* murals with classical scenes in the style of Piranesi, painted on two facing walls by an itinerant Italian artist passing through the Pennsylvania region at that time.

There were dark hardwood floors throughout the house, including the ballroom floor, further adorned with a delicate floral design marble inset at its center. Two large mirrors at either end of this special room created a sense of even greater space; against one of these mirrored walls, Rosalia would eventually place an antique French clock and garniture on a long classical style console table—that and several small gilt chairs and a piano being the only furniture. The chairs would provide seating for musicians when Rosalia arranged a little musicale or a small party for dancing, either to elegant waltzes or the latest Jazz Age fast numbers in 4/4 time—the Charleston and the fashionable fox trot.

Upstairs were six bedrooms and three baths. The third floor, partly unfinished, was accessible from a backstairs and had a large cedar closet, trunk room and a little apartment for a servant who could enjoy the view of the surrounding mountains from the roof's dormer windows.

Rosalia and Federico made several trips to Pittsburgh to purchase materials for draperies and upholstery, oriental rugs, tapestries for the library, and a great deal of furniture. From a relative of Francesco living in Naples, Rosalia also was able to obtain the address and catalogue of a famous artisan house specializing in the production of *passementerie*: elegant and unusual tassels, fringes, shade pulls and other ornamental pieces.

Later, for the layout of the garden, they consulted with a local landscape architect. Rosalia provided a sketch of a small formal section she envisioned: a long, somewhat narrow, sunken area of lawn, with a fountain centered in a small bricked square, set with four statues representing the seasons, and bordered by raised beds to be planted with varieties of annual and perennial flowers. For closing the view at the far end, the architect proposed a small neo-classical pavilion, a pump or spring house constructed in a brick matching that of the house. This formal garden was to be set to the side of the house, adjacent to the conservatory, rather than at the rear of the property. The immense windows of the conservatory or solarium (with its interior of trellises and a small island of tropical plants; and sometime later, a colorful but ill-tempered parrot!) would look directly on to it; it would also be partially visible from the street.

Federico hoped to fulfill his own dream of planting fruit trees, a little orchard of ten or so apple and pear trees on one side of the house, and a similar number of cherry and peach trees on the other, behind the pump house. He also desired to set aside a more private area for a secret garden that eventually would have a shrine dedicated to St. Joseph, the patron saint of Sicily. In anticipation of this little hermitage (to be set at a short distance from the rear of the house), mountain rhododendrons were planted early on as a border for a quincunx-shaped court, defined by clipped boxwood and flagstone pathways. At some future time, a statue or other representation of the saint would occupy the middle of the court. A tiny herb garden was also set in close proximity to the house's kitchen door and basement trapdoor.

The enormous basement was accessible inside from two stairwells, one close to the *porte cochere* entry, and the other directly from the kitchen. The area was divided for several purposes: a coal furnace with bins; a kitchen with a very large stove, oversized icebox and counterspace for canning; a place for storing bulbs, potting and arranging flowers; and last, but not least, a very generous space for maintaining the apparatus and barrels for making and storing wine. Federico had observed the making of wine many times in Sicily. In a few years, he would be able to do so on his own, with choice grapes ordered from California and a special variety of muscat just beginning to be cultivated in the picturesque vineyards he had purchased in the New York Finger Lakes region.

Federico was known to own several large warehousing properties both in town and on the outskirts. Therefore, it came as no surprise when, during the turbulent years of Prohibition, he was approached two or three times by bootleggers seeking such facilities for their highly profitable operations. However, he flatly refused to align himself with either compromising "pillars of the community," certain unscrupulous politicians or other patently unsavory criminal types. A lesser man may have given in to the temptation. Federico chose the narrow, upright path because of his strong sense of personal honor, the value he placed on his hard-earned, honest accomplishments, and his concern to protect the integrity and unsullied reputation of his name and family.

(The struggle between the reformist and temperance "dry" groups who opposed the real and perceived evils of "saloon culture," and the "wet" camps who considered restriction on alcohol as unreasonable, foolish or stupid, and therefore unenforceable, eventually ended in legislation that had unforeseen, disastrous economic consequences: the undoing of the country's fifth largest industry—the thousand or more successful, legitimate breweries, with the loss of many thousands of jobs. And this, at a most inopportune time of impending national financial crisis!

Later, after Repeal, Pennsylvania would maintain strict controls on the marketing, sale and consumption of alcoholic beverages.)

THE MOVE   On the day of the move,
1926   Rosalia dressed   the
children in brightly colored summerwear. For herself, she chose a favorite sundress, and for her husband, very comfortable casuals. Everyone was beaming with excitement and anticipation.

After they arrived at the house and admired its impressive aspect, the children rushed in, running from room to room, eventually going upstairs to check out their individual bedrooms. Federico detained Rosalia downstairs, bringing her attention to little details, first in the entry, then in the living room and ballroom. He had a plan he didn't want upset.

Within a few minutes, right on cue, one could hear noise, something gasping and rumbling on the crushed stone of the driveway. It was a small truck with no markings. Rosalia said to Federico – "Are we expecting something for delivery? All the furniture, at least for now, is here in place. Is something missing?" "Oh, I think something *is* missing," Federico said emphatically. At that, the doorbell rang. Pretending to be occupied with something, Federico asked Rosalia if she could see who was there. When she opened the door, a truckman said, "Misses D'Argenti? We have your piano, Madam." Rosalia stepped back speechless. She turned around to Federico with astonishment. His face was flushed, brimming with adoring love and a broad smile of mischievous pleasure.

She had been content playing an

old, fairly decent upright in the apartment all those years. Now, within a matter of a half-hour, a beautiful art case grand piano was uncrated and positioned in her elegant ballroom.

"Do you like it?" Federico asked. Tearfully, Rosalia responded, "I love it, it is simply beautiful! How sweet and sneaky of you, darling," as she kissed him on his cheek. With the children now sharing in the excitement of this wonderful surprise, Rosalia sat down, rested and then arched her long, fine and delicate hands on the keyboard and began to play Federico's favorite piece, Elgar's "Salut d'Amour." Though not proposed at the moment, the children both faced the prospect of many more lessons and hours of practice on this superior instrument!

(In later years, Federico would often sit alone in the ballroom at twilight, gazing at the piano and recalling his wife's delight and pleasure in playing.

He believed with all his heart that her music had sweetened the very timber of the house and that anyone visiting could sense the special joy and golden glow that once engulfed this lovely room and caressed those favored to be there.)

Finally freed from all the responsibilities at the downtown business, Rosalia could now recast her special *art de vivre* and be a true lady of leisure, devoting her attention to the gracious running of this new household and fostering her favorite charities. Federico had already established stylish new office quarters on the hill to conduct his several ventures, while, at the same time, enjoying the benefit of close proximity to his new home.

Rosalia would soon earn a reputation as a vibrant and peerless hostess. Over the years, she would plan many memorable events—celebrations of all kinds for the children, especially their birthdays and graduations, as well as several benefit luncheons and dinners. At holiday time, friends and acquaintances would look forward to attending her parties in the ballroom, with music and dancing, or little plays or poetry readings by writers and authors Federico and she counted among their many accomplished friends.

The most elaborate affair would be Fabrizio's rehearsal dinner, with the entire property—house and garden—glimmering with candles and torches, all set to the strains of violin and piano music. The most memorable musical evening of all would be when Francesco arranged for his personal friend, the acclaimed Italian American opera star, Josephine Lucchese Donato, to give a private recital while on her way to Chicago and her national tour.

The next morning's Pittsburgh chronicle headlined, "The 'American Nightingale' Sings at D'Argenti's." (After her American and European tour, the lovely *cantatrice* Donato returned to become the leading coloratura soprano of the Philadelphia Grand Opera Company).

THE BOMB
AND
THE HONOR
1926

Two months or so had passed since their move. It was supposed to be an especially happy day, but there was an unseasonal chill in the air this mid-October morning. At breakfast, Rosalia reminded Federico that she had already laid out a special shirt and tie to go with his favorite business suit. She herself would soon be attired in a smart new outfit for the special occasion. The children were to remain home in the care of Rina, their new maid, a nineteen-year old girl, whose family came from a little town near Venice in northern Italy.

138

At mid-morning, Rina rushed into the library where Federico was taking his second cup of coffee and reading the paper. In a panic-stricken voice, she blurted out – "Mister D'Argenti, I just went to the mailbox and there's an awful, strange looking thing in there." "What do you mean?" said Federico. "Is it an animal?" "Oh, I don't know, I've never seen anything like it; it has a very funny shape." And she began to cry. "Take it easy, Rina, I'll go and see for myself."

Federico approached the box and opened it carefully. He saw what appeared to be a crude explosive with a folded piece of paper next to it. Rushing back to the house, he told Rosalia to call the authorities. When the police chief arrived with his squad, the note was gingerly removed. The chief scowled as he read it and then passed it on to Federico. It read – "Who do you think you are, you wop! We don't want you foreigners here. Go back to where you came from, or else."

Federico was upset, but in a way, not entirely surprised. Years earlier, he had experienced a similar situation at the store, and just recently, as he and Rosalia were reviewing the detailed deed to their new property, they had come upon a shocking and disturbing entry: a restrictive covenant forbidding sale to certain named groups. Oddly, it had no exclusionary clause or proscription regarding Italians. Perhaps those who were responsible for this, Federico thought, never imagined that Italians would ever be capable of purchasing the land, otherwise they might have been similarly targeted for exclusion.

The police chief promised Federico that he would conduct a thorough investigation. He assured him that, in the meanwhile, he would provide surveillance of the property for an indefinite period. Before he left, however, he asked a strange question. He said, "Mister D'Argenti, do you know of anyone who would envy or resent you enough to threaten you?" This struck Federico as odd, but got him to thinking what sinister forces might be at work. He wondered if the rebuffed bootleggers or possibly the "Black Hand" might be sending a warning or threat of something truly real and worse!

The next day's local newspaper featured a front-page article and picture, "Federico D'Argenti Honored as Business Man of the Year," and, in the second section, a small report on the bottom corner of a page entitled, "Bomb Threat in Bluff Hills," with no mention of any name or address.

The bomb turned out to be bogus. No one responsible for the incident was ever found. No other threat was ever forthcoming.

THE
MAUSOLEUM
1928

The growing Roman Catholic population, largely of younger immigrant stock, was beginning to move into several districts surrounding the core or old center of the city.

A middle-aged, portly priest, Father Francis Moretti, newly assigned to the diocesan development office, had been advised by the bishop to talk to Federico, a man recognized as one of the most prominent Catholics in the area. The principal concern of the bishop was to secure reasonably priced land on which to build a new church to be dedicated to Our Lady of Mount Carmel. This situation was a bit unusual since, in most instances, diocesan needs of this kind were planned very far in advance, often decades.

Although a practical and capable man with very wide administrative experience, Father Moretti approached Federico with some apprehension, if not mild timidity. However, to his delight, the meeting in Federico's office was immediately cordial; the two men felt a special affinity. Father's family, from the Puglia region of Italy, had originally settled in West Virginia, but the ties of relatives and old friends had brought them here.

When Father Moretti disclosed the reason for requesting to meet, Federico, without any hesitation, proposed to donate the land. Astonished, Father Moretti said – "Have I understood correctly, Mister D'Argenti? Did you say you would *donate* the land?" "Yes, Father, with one condition, that you would plan to incorporate a cemetery with consecrated ground within the complex." "I'm sure the bishop will approve, Mister D'Argenti."

As Father got into his little Model A coupe, he whispered reverently, "Thank you, dear Madonna of Mount Carmel, your church is on its way." When Bishop

Boyle, the son of Irish immigrants, received Father Moretti's good news, he exclaimed in a lilting brogue, "The saints be praised, they sent an angel in the person of this dear Mister D'Argenti!"

As expected, Federico chaired the building committee (and would eventually serve as a member of the first church council). Without delay, as the church was going up, Federico first consulted with his friend, Rinaldo, in Washington, and then employed his architect and workmen to construct a mausoleum in a lovely shaded spot in the designated cemetery area.

When complete, the mausoleum looked like it could last forever. The exterior was entirely of stone; each stone was individually shaped by two stonecutters who hailed from Lombardy, and set in place by two meticulous German masons. Similar to the mansion, it had a slate roof and copper fittings.

Although simply designed on

the exterior, the interior was laid out elaborately with costly materials. There were ten crypts in all. Federico planned for the interment of himself and Rosalia, his son and his spouse and, for the more distant future, perhaps their children as well. The entire inside—floor, slabs fronting the crypts, an altar for the celebration of mass, and even the ceiling— was of white Carrara marble. A stained-glass window depicting Christ in the Garden of Gethsemane was set above the altar. A solid glass door, attached to an intricate wrought iron gate, admitted soft light into the interior. Over the door, on the exterior, a thick limestone lintel was carved with the name, "D'Argenti."

Federico had ordered a great quantity of uncut stone, much more than was needed for the mausoleum. This he saved. When the time came to build a grand Tudor-style home as a wedding present for his son, Fabrizio, and his wife, Cecilia, he hired the same artisans who prepared the stones and set them together with intricate herringbone brick patterns on the mansion's façade.

ST. JOSEPH 1928   March came in gently like a lamb. One morning, out of the blue, Rosalia received a call from Rinaldo in Washington. After some pleasantries, he asked if she and Federico would like some company. It had been a while since their last get-together. Responding with delight, she asked—"Are the children coming with you?" Rosalia hoped it would be the case so that Fabrizio and Giulietta, both now teenagers, could renew their childhood friendships. She knew that Fabrizio would be especially pleased to spend some time with his godfather whose occupation he found very interesting, and his lively, engaging personality, attractive and lots of fun.

"Yes, Rosalia", said Rinaldo, "they will be coming, but we have a problem. We have another little one we would like to bring along. He won't take much room – We'll explain when we see you. Will that be all right?"

"Rinaldo, you know our home is always wide open to you and Matilda. Federico and I won't be able to sleep until you get here! Just have a safe trip; the mountain roads can be very slippery this time of year. When can we expect you?"

"We're thinking of arriving on the eve of St. Joseph's feastday."

"Oh, that's wonderful," replied Rosalia, "Perhaps I can prepare a little St. Joseph's table; I think the children would like that."

Right after Rinaldo's call, Rosalia rang Francesco and Elena in Pittsburgh,

147

proposing that they come too and surprise the Marsellis. However, it was going to be an exam period just before the college's spring recess and, unfortunately, Francesco was not going to be able to break away. Even though the families visited each other rather frequently, Giulietta was deeply disappointed that her godparents could not come this time and be part of the special religious celebration.

The 18th of March brought a brush of light snow but the sun shone most of the morning and into the late afternoon. Around four-thirty, Federico heard the noisy approach of a car in the driveway. Looking out the front door, he remarked to Rosalia – "It's odd, the car has some strange contraption attached to its back end. It's sticking out. What could it be? I know Rinaldo has turned to fishing for a pastime, but he can't possibly be thinking of doing such at this time of year, could he? It's warm in Washington now but here the rivers and streams are still half-frozen."

They both rushed out to welcome and hug and kiss their friends; the children trailed closely behind. It had been a very long, trying trip—the Marsellis looked exhausted. As they drew near, Rinaldo quickly stepped in front of the makeshift-looking attachment to the muddy car in an effort to conceal something. Curious, Federico attempted to peer over his shoulder. "What's that?" queried Federico. "Oh," said Rinaldo, "that's the 'little one' I told Rosalia we wanted to bring." With that, he snapped off a padded blanket. There, in a prone position, was a marble statue of St. Joseph.

"Caro amico," said Rinaldo, "You told me over the phone several months ago that you still hadn't created the shrine

you wanted in your garden, only that you had some masons build and install a base for a statue. "I've rendered this for you with all my heart and soul. I hope you like it."

Deeply moved, Federico embraced his friend, saying—"How can I ever thank you, *compare*?" Rosalia, with tearful eyes, added – "It's so beautiful, Rinaldo. Every time we look at it and pray before it, we will be reminded of you and your kindness."

The statue was truly extraordinary and far from the more conventional, highly stylized or formal byzantine versions commonly seen: St. Joseph standing very straight and looking forward, while at the same time, supporting the Christ Child on his left arm and holding a long-stem lily with his right hand.

Rinaldo's conception was full of charm: St. Joseph was still supporting Jesus with his left arm, but with two fingers of his right hand, he appeared to be lightly squeezing or pinching the little child's left cheek. Jesus seemed to be responding with his tiny mouth slightly open, as if he were laughing or being tickled. At the bottom of the statue, Rinaldo had carved a bed of lilies on which St. Joseph appeared to be pausing or coming to a rest. Nestled close to the saint's feet was an endearing little dog.

After continuing to admire the statue for a little while, the ladies and the children, with the exception of Giulietta, entered the house. Giulietta lingered for a few minutes, reverently touching the statue while seeming to offer a prayer. The men moved to the garden where they determined how to position and secure the statue to the base. Before long, Rosalia called them inside to freshen up for dinner.

The next morning, Rosalia, Rina and Matilda—with the children anxious to help, and Buffi, the new puppy, running underfoot—began preparing a traditional St. Joseph's Table. Rosalia had invited other friends, Federico's business associates and their families, as well as several close neighbors, to attend the event scheduled for the very late afternoon and early evening.

A week or so before, Federico had had a carpenter build a tall stepped platform to sit atop a large table placed against one of the walls of the ballroom. The ladies now draped the table and steps with fine linen cloths on which they artfully placed variously shaped breads and delicate, colorfully decorated little cakes, a few bright oranges and lemons, green herbs, dried palms, fresh flowers in vases, and votive and other tall white and ivory candles. From the morning and into mid-afternoon, they prepared generous portions of light meatless fare, including many unusual vegetable and fish dishes, special pastas and traditional Sicilian desserts. The tasks seemed light, inspired by love and devotion.

At the table's official opening and blessing, Rosalia and Federico would be expected to invite the young children of their neighbors or friends to join Giulietta and Fabrizio in representing the Holy Family, the Apostles and angels. Following pious tradition, they would be sure that all these "saintly" and "angelic" children were the first to be served.

At five o'clock, right on cue, Father Moretti rushed in to bless the table and the people present. Soon after, he was shown the statue, Rinaldo's gift, which the men and Chad, the recently hired caretaker, had carefully secured on its base in the

153

garden. Father marveled at its unique conception, saying—"Isn't it wonderful to represent the Christ Child giggling or laughing? It shows such tender human feeling between St. Joseph and his little Son. What a talent God has given you, Rinaldo, a talent which happily you share so generously with others."

With that, Father invoked another benediction on the statue, its creator and all present, including—to the surprise and delight of the young people—a special blessing on Buffi, the new puppy. Father had thought to himself—"There is no mention of pets in the Gospels, but given the convincing way Rinaldo has portrayed the saint, it is very likely that St. Joseph provided his precious Child with a little pet for companionship. My own baptismal name is Francis, and my saintly patron, the sweet, gentle man from Assisi, who loved and preached to God's little creatures, would warmly approve this!"

The day the Marsellis chose to depart began with a heavy fog typical of mornings in the hill district. Rosalia rose before dawn to prepare a box lunch for their long trip. Federico, still earlier, had been able to sneak in the back seat of their car, a box filled with Italian staples and a large bunch of bright yellow bananas he had brought home fresh from the refrigerated rooms of his warehouse the day before.

As they were leaving, Rinaldo opened his car window and said – *"San Giuseppe vi benedica sempre, carissimi!"* ("May St. Joseph bless you always, dearest friends!")

With that, they drove off. Rosalia, Federico and the half-awake, blurry-eyed children waved until they no longer could see the car through the slowly lifting mist.

The "little one," now safely ensconced in its new home, would be admired and loved by all who would see it.

Part Four
1939 - 1940

THE PRINCE'S
DEATH
1939

For some unexplainable reason, Federico had not been himself for a few days. On this particular morning, his attitude should have improved for it was unusually bright, with the sun illuminating every room of the house. Even when he went to his beautifully remodeled offices at his industrial park on the hill, he felt that nothing seemed to be going right. Frustrated, he left earlier than usual, hoping to convince Rosalia to go out for a light supper at a restaurant along the river basin. He desperately needed a change of scene. Perhaps it would improve his gloomy mood. This was not to be the case.

As Federico entered the front hall, he saw Rosalia writing at her desk in the library—she seemed pensive. Rearranging the sleeve on her right wrist and pushing back an errant tress of her hair, she came forward with an envelope. Handing it to him, she said – "*Caro*, this letter has sad news. It was addressed just to you but I opened it, it looked important."

Taking the letter, Federico recognized the return, even though it was partially smudged. Nervously, he opened it. It read:

Noto, Sicily
12 April 1939

Dear Federico,

I am sorry to have to write you this but I am certain you would want to know. Our dear Prince Fabrizio Bronte di Terranova-Chiaravalle passed away two weeks ago after a brief illness. Most of us had been unaware of the seriousness of his condition.

Those attending him said that his passing was peaceful except that at the last moment he seemed agitated, as if he wished to convey something, someone's name perhaps, but was much too weak to do so. What may have been troubling him, we shall probably never know.

I am reluctant to admit that the future of his remaining estate is very uncertain, especially his beloved Casa, the palace. A few years ago, he was forced to sell his townhouse in Palermo and the seaside retreat outside Catania, retaining only the palace here and the family's ancestral castle near Agrigento. More heart-breaking for all involved, however, was his need to dismiss most of his old loyal household staff. For quite a while now, the palace has been functioning with the barest of personnel and resources. Undoubtedly, before long it will lapse into total insolvency. The times have brought serious financial problems and his generous philanthropies, over the years, virtually emptied his treasury. He was a proud man who never would have contemplated seeking any assistance.

Though he was, as you may remember, a very private person, he did share with us, from time to time, news about you and your life in America, from the letters he received from you. I would mention, parenthetically, that up until her death a few years ago, dear Mariannina also used to give us news about you whenever you sent her letters and thoughtful packages of gifts and money for which, by the way, she was always most grateful. Poor soul, after the tragic death of her daughter, Viviana, in a terrible auto accident on the Amalfi Road, she was never quite the same cheerful and happy person we all had known.

As I am sure you have always been aware, Federico, the prince had a very special regard for you and referred to you with special affection in all the years of your absence. Given his passing, I am now free to reveal to you that he had planned to leave you a remembrance, but alas, his intended bequest has virtually vanished with the tragic collapse of his fortune.

Simple religious services were held here in Noto. In Palermo, however, there was a civic observance at the opera house which included a moving orchestral tribute by many of those young musicians he had sponsored over the years and who have become highly accomplished and acclaimed artists. It was truly an impressive memorial, conducted with the magnificence and dignity befitting a great man. A solemn procession to his interment in the family crypt followed.

May his soul rest in peace.

My esteem,
Nicola Giuffré
Chief Accountant

After a light supper which he barely ate, Federico went to sit in the library where he lingered in the dark until bedtime. Rosalia respected his need to be alone. She thought to herself – "Perhaps this is the reason Federico has been 'out-of-sorts' these past few days."

THE ANNIVERSARY The house on 1940 stately East Bluff Boulevard was all resplendent. In her typical way, Rosalia had seen to every detail. She had ordered several flower arrangements, making sure they included some of Federico's favorites; to these she added some flowers that were blooming at the time in her own cutting gardens. She also requested several tall topiary pieces from the florist to accent and add a touch of drama to the ballroom. She placed beautiful linen cloths on the several round dining tables provided for the fifty or so expected guests; the main buffet table she draped with her finest cloth, one she had made with the aid of the Ursuline sisters in Sicily so many years before.

Federico had hired waiters from a local hotel to assist the caterers. Rina had been polishing silver and furniture for the past two weeks, and Chad, the caretaker, had make certain that everything in the gardens was mulched, trimmed and manicured to perfection. Even old Buff, the sweet-natured and often over-friendly yellow retriever, got a special grooming and a big green ribbon which, oddly, he didn't resist.

Federico came home very early from his office to see if he could help with some last minute details. Rosalia looked a little drawn and pale. Knowing how fastidious she was, he thought she was probably just nervous or anxious.

It was their thirtieth wedding anniversary.

As they were getting ready, Rosalia asked Federico to help her with the buttons on the back of her evening dress. He had been waiting for her customary request. As he assisted her, he slipped a brilliant emerald and diamond necklace on her. It looked stunning with the tight-waisted, ankle-length dress she had chosen, made of shimmering celadon taffeta with a simple bodice, low round open neckline and a side sash with cascading folds.

Rosalia immediately began to tear up, saying – "Federico, I am just so grateful that we could celebrate this special day with all our family and friends. To have you is enough to make me the happiest woman on this earth. You are always so thoughtful and caring, darling." As she fashioned her hair in a chignon, she adjusted the necklace's position and admired it in the mirror. Now composed, she turned to him – "I love this gift! It's so gorgeous. I hope the way it looks on me pleases you." Looking at her approvingly, Federico replied, "Even with the simplest of raiment, dearest, you adorn my world. I live only for you, without you I am nothing."

After putting on diamond stud earrings she felt complemented her beautiful gift, she quickly opened a drawer of her vanity and removed a small black velvet box. In it was a large ring which she had designed and her jeweler had rendered. It was of white gold, set with a large onyx to which was affixed, also in etched white gold, a small figure of the Medusa or Trinacria, the symbol of Sicily. As Federico opened the box, he exclaimed, "What a marvelous present! How did you ever think of something like this?" Then, for just a fleeting moment, seeming to suppress some disturbing, dark presentiment, he added – "This is really extraordinary, darling, but I want you to know that you will always be my choicest jewel." Taking her hand, he kissed it and pressed it close to his cheek.

Soon they could hear the first lovely strains of orchestra music in the ballroom below.

Smiling brightly and looking regal, Rosalia touched some perfume lightly to her wrists and neck and placed her arm in his, as he said – "Now let's go downstairs, my treasure, and welcome our guests."

The affair was unsurpassed by any that had come before or would come thereafter.

THE DARKEST DAY The guests had 1940 all given their goodbyes, including the elderly banker, Mister Norton, and his wife, Lydia, and Rinaldo and Matilda, who really wished to remain, but instead had to travel all night to return to Washington for a family engagement. Fabrizio was already on his way back from returning Giulietta and her companion sister to the convent in Wilkinsburg. Daughter-in-law Cecilia had left early to return home to little Christopher who had made a brief appearance at the party but was now in the care of a babysitter.

The caterers straightened out the kitchen and ballroom and packed their wares. Likewise, the musicians tucked their instruments and music stands in their cars and departed.

An exhausted but content Rina, who had taken charge of all the operations in the kitchen (including the waiters!), climbed slowly up the steep stairs to her little apartment.

Their friends, Francesco and Elena, who were staying overnight, lingered a while to talk and wind down. Eventually, they gave their affectionate embraces and goodnight and went up to their room.

Federico and Rosalia, weary but pleased with how all had gone so beautifully, decided that it was time to retire to their bedroom as well. As they passed through the entry hall to ascend the stairs, they were surprised to see many fancily wrapped and beribboned gifts piled high on top and beneath the round table in the center of the room. As she glanced admiringly at the colorful array of boxes, Rosalia exclaimed – "Oh no! Our friends chose to ignore our request not to bring presents! But I'm so terribly tired, Federico, we'll have to leave it to tomorrow to open them. That way, Francesco and Elena, the children, and Rina too, can join us in the fun and suspense. We must do it carefully, when I'm wide awake, so that I can remember to send appropriate thank-you's."

Stifling a yawn, Federico merely nodded a quiet assent and extended his hand to her to go up the stairs.

Federico got in bed first, but he could hear the rustle of satin as Rosalia disrobed in her dressing room. When she joined him, he held her close. Stroking her flowing hair tenderly, he told her how proud he was of her, how radiant she had looked, of the beautiful children she had given him, and how she blessed his every day with her sweetness and kindness. She kissed him delicately, whispering in his ear, "I love you so much, Federico." They embraced and quickly fell off to sleep, softly entwined in the lavender-scented linens of their luxurious bed.

It had been a long while since Federico needed to rise early as in the first years of the banana business, now more than a quarter of a century ago. This morning it was especially welcome and delicious to linger. Normally, Rosalia would already be up, attending to the many things that usually had her attention. Some mornings, to Federico's delight, she would slip into the ballroom before breakfast and play some lovely piece on the piano.

However, this morning she was still next to him, taking, he thought, a little extra time after such an exhausting day before. He touched her and she seemed very cool; he spoke her name, but she didn't respond. Jumping out of the bed and racing down the hallway, he yelled downstairs to Rina who was already in the kitchen – "Rina, something is wrong with Misses D'Argenti. Call Doctor Chiappetta right away! And an ambulance, quickly!" In the meanwhile, with tears running down his face, he kept calling her name, petting her hands and forehead, and telling her repeatedly that help would come soon. Rosalia was unresponsive.

Arriving minutes before the ambulance, Doctor Chiappetta, their close friend and neighbor, raced up the long stairway. In the brief moment it took to examine Rosalia, he said in a soft voice, "My friend, Federico, your dear wife is gone."

Francesco and Elena were still sleeping in one of the guest bedrooms at the opposite end of the house and had heard none of the commotion. The ambulance hadn't sounded a siren. Now Rina, ghostly pale and shivering, walked the long hall and knocked gently on their door. When Elena opened the door, she said simply, in a barely audible voice – "Misses D'Argenti has passed away."

Elena fell back into the room, half-faint. Steadying herself on the arm of a nearby chair, she shrieked at the top of her lungs. "No! No! No! Rosalia is gone? It can't be! It can't be! Francesco, release me from this horrible dream!" Rushing forward, Francesco was at a loss to quiet or comfort her. She began sobbing and wailing uncontrollably, repeating – "How could this be? How could this be? She looked so healthy, so beautiful last night. O my dear, sweet friend, Rosalia, Rosalia! O God, O God, poor Federico, what will he do, what will he do?"

The day of the funeral, Federico, weak with grief, could barely walk and had to be assisted by Fabrizio. Giulietta had returned from the convent with a large group of sisters who joined the choir of the church at the high mass concelebrated by the bishop, Father Moretti, and several other priests whom Federico and Rosalia had befriended over the years. Giulietta attended her father and tried to comfort him but he seemed unaware of what was taking place. In his mind, he kept cursing the day he decided to build the mausoleum, saying to himself, "I was supposed to be the first one to be placed there, not my dear Rosalia." When the bishop came forward to bless the coffin with holy water and incense and to intone the moving farewell prayer, "May the angels greet you at your coming….," — Federico turned completely ashen and nearly collapsed.

After the reception at home that ran late into the afternoon, Federico went up to the bedroom where he sat most of the night gazing at Rosalia's picture. Not even for a second did old Buff move away from Federico's feet. Every now and then, he looked up and whimpered—a sympathetic lament for his master's sorrow.

For some good reasons, Fabrizio strongly objected, but then agreed to Federico's insistence that Rosalia be interred wearing the necklace he had just given her. True, it was a mere material thing, but Federico felt it would help assuage his grief to remember her as she looked on their special anniversary day and not in her final moments when he felt so utterly helpless. Furthermore, he could never picture the necklace on another woman.

Rosalia's sudden and unexpected death had the sting of indifferent and unjust earthly finality. As the flower in her name, a rose—with some of its sweetest petals yet folded—she had lived brightly for the mere duration of a morning in the midsummer of life. As best as he could, Federico tried to find consolation in the thought that their love was sublimely cloistered somewhere in an imperishable spiritual realm—eternal and triumphant.

Yet, there still were terrible moments, he candidly admitted to Father

Moretti, when he questioned and even rebuked God. "Why," he thought, "did God take away such a kind and good soul while He permitted so many evil and hateful people to go on living? Why would He deprive many of someone so capable of loving others and bringing them happiness?"

In his golden orrery, safe in its library cabinet, the sun would keep its central place among the orbiting planets. In Federico's earthly life now, his sun was gone forever; his world had gone cold as ice. Without Rosalia's sweet and loving presence, how would he endure?

Many weeks later, when he had regained a measure of the will to carry on, he had carved on her crypt:

"Like the sun, her love radiated
and warmed into life
and beauty, all she touched"

Book Two

Part One
1935 - 1964

THE GRANDSONS   It was no secret.
1935, 1943   From his youth,
Federico and Rosalia's only son, Fabrizio,
had an issue about "being American."
When it came to dating and marriage, he
either was not familiar with, or more likely
just plainly chose to ignore, the rather
well-known Italian maxim that advised
one "to seek merchandise or a wife from
one's own town," meaning figuratively,
to acquire something of value from one's
own culture or people.

To the dismay of his parents,
Fabrizio never even attempted to date,
much less court, a girl of Italian descent,

even though there were many attractive possibilities. Instead, he dated several girls of different nationalities and eventually married a stunning redhead, Cecilia McGraw, from an accomplished Irish American family. Fabrizio and she had two sons, Christopher and Roland.

Christopher was named after Cecilia's father. Not surprisingly, Fabrizio had refused to observe the old Italian custom of naming one's first-born son or any son, for that matter, after one's father or grandfather. Of course, Federico was disappointed. However, he finessed somewhat of a minor victory very early on, by calling his younger grandson by his Italian name, Orlando. And, to his delight and satisfaction, it prevailed!

Christopher, the older boy, always seemed to please his father. In Fabrizio's

eyes, he could never do wrong. He seemed
born with an entrepreneurial spirit. From
the earliest, he liked handling money,
whether it was the penny change from his
impromptu lemonade stand or the thrill of
depositing the gift of a fresh five-dollar
bill into his bank account. To Fabrizio's
liking, this son showed great interest in
business affairs; in time he would choose
an educational path that would be an asset
to the family's financial interests. While
studying law at Cornell University, he
dated a graduate student in the School of
Child Development, Cynthia Harrington,
from Mobile, Alabama. Upon graduating,
they married.

Roland, that is, Orlando, was
happiest with his head in a book. As a
mere toddler playing with crayons, and
later as a teen progressing to pen and

brush, he also loved to depict objects, sketch a little scene, or merely scribble unusual and decorative doodles in the margins of his books. He had an unusual gift, as well, for fashioning fanciful things from diverse, often discarded, remnants of paper, wood, cloth or other. Highly imaginative, yet retiring and meditative, he had all the makings of a future artist or designer, perhaps even a serious scholar— in all likelihood, given these early bents, an art historian or a museum curator.

Although it came as no surprise that Fabrizio was deeply disappointed and did not attempt to conceal his antipathy toward his younger son's interests, it was, admittedly, a rather puzzling, if not somewhat ironic situation. In his youth, Fabrizio had found his godfather Rinaldo's work as a sculptor fascinating and even an attractive calling; and now, in adulthood, he was also an artist himself, a fine pianist. Yet, he constantly berated Cecilia   for encouraging the boy's artistic inclinations and defending his bookish behavior. With his face framed in tense lines, he would often complain— "I know the boy is going to be a drifter. He lives in the proverbial ivory tower. He'll never amount to anything." Then, in a still more accusatory fashion— with the edge of anger in his voice—he'd shout, "It's that Jesuit brother of yours and his friend, Professor Jim Geraci, and all his brainy, egghead cronies who feed his imagination with stories about the glories of Italy and all her arts. You know perfectly well I want Orlando in the business. And where does he want to go? To the ruins of some God-forsaken place or to some old, smelly museum! Such nonsense! He should be preparing to go to Wharton!"

Although he respectfully left the matter unspoken, Fabrizio also deeply resented his father Federico's influence on Orlando, filling the young boy's head with all things Sicilian.

Cecilia would quietly suffer Fabrizio's tirades while, at the same time, reassuring her studious, handsome son that all would be well. She would say, "Orlando, don't fret. Your dad will come around some day." Then, invariably, she would quote one of her favorite Irish proverbs – "There's not a tree in heaven higher than the tree of patience."

If Federico were present at one of these distressing episodes, he would chime in with the ancient axiom of Ovid, "All from the same womb, but not of the same mind." Then, attempting to pour honey and mollify the harsh and bitter atmosphere, he would add, in a very gentle tone of voice, almost a whisper— "Why not let the boy follow his loves and interests? In the end, that brings true happiness and success."

The older boy, Christopher, of course, loved and respected his grandfather, but it was the so-called dreamer, Orlando, who, from his earliest years, would seek out his grandfather's company over and over again. There was some unmistakable *simpatia* between the two.

"Grandpa Fede"—as both the boys affectionately called Federico, a respectful play on his Sicilian childhood sobriquet—would regale Orlando with stories about his early life in Sicily, his service to the prince, how he met and fell in love with Rosalia, the excitement of the crossing of the Atlantic and his beginnings in America. He would also describe what grandmother Rosalia was like (she had died just two years before his birth) and the many beauties of Sicily— its spectacular sea coasts and fiery Mount Etna, its wonderful ancient temples, its medieval castles and monasteries.

As a little fellow, Orlando especially enjoyed listening to his grandfather's fascinating tales of the knights of the Crusades as they once had been recounted by the loving Sicilian storyteller, Mariannina. Naturally, he was particularly fond of the legends of Orlando or Roland, the knight with whom he shared the name.

One day when he was only about six years old, he took strong objection to an episode in which his hero lost his love, Angelica, to another knight. He instantly blurted out—"That's not the way it should be, Grandpa! When I grow up, no one will steal my girl!"

Federico couldn't help but laugh at the little tyke's earnest protest. He was amused and pleased too that his little grandson showed such spirit and spunk. He thought to himself – "Fabrizio might someday be very surprised at what this boy will accomplish."

From the time when he would sit on his grandfather's lap, walk hand-in-hand with him in the garden or, when older, just sit to converse at the table after dinner, Orlando never tired of hearing about this enchanting place called Sicily. The highlight and special treat of many of the very early times together would be to look at and touch the golden orrery which Federico displayed in a special cabinet in the library. He loved looking at it and making the planets spin in their orbits. It had a certain magical attraction and, as he grew older, he believed that perhaps it held some mystery that one day might be revealed to him.

For Federico, these pleasant encounters with his endearing little grandson with the luminous green eyes, never failed to remind him of his beloved spouse. It served as a gentle balm.

Orlando often asked about his grandmother. He seemed especially happy to learn that she had been instructed in drawing by the Sicilian sisters and that perhaps he had inherited the love of art and ability to design from her. As he grew older, he enjoyed countless times quietly perusing the many beautifully illustrated art books, especially the old nineteenth century commentaries, his grandmother had collected for her personal library.

By the time Orlando entered his teens, he became attuned and very sensitive to his grandfather's moods more than any other family member. He recognized Federico's ever-deepening nostalgia for his past far from the American shores. It was something, he realized, that probably had begun to set in almost imperceptibly, slowly and softly--- like a *crescendo poco a poco--* soon after his loss of Rosalia. Orlando perceived, as well, his grandfather's disappointment that he would never have the blessing and joy of knowing his wonderful grandmother personally.

When the time came for college, Orlando chose studies in classical literature at Columbia University. Sometime soon after graduating with honors from this program, he decided to pursue another degree in architecture at Harvard. This rather unusual progression of interests was inspired by his attendance at an event at the Italian Cultural Institute on New York's Park Avenue: a fascinating presentation on Sicilian baroque architecture. During the elegant reception following, Orlando had the opportunity to meet and briefly visit with the engaging speaker, the renowned British art historian, Sir Anthony Blunt, who informed him that, within the next year or two, he planned to publish an extensive photographic commentary on Sicily's unique and beautiful baroque heritage.

At this point in Orlando's life, it seemed many of his interests, stemming from way back in childhood, were gathering into some uniquely personal entity or force. Indeed, the Fates were already busy at work, for all this would eventually lead to something in Orlando's future, something unanticipated but mysteriously foreordained.

Part Two
1965 - 1967

THE DEMISE   Federico's   mind for
      1965   business   was   never
at rest. Over the years, he often quoted
his favorite Italian proverb to both his
line and management employees: *"Chi
non risica, non rosica"* – "Nothing
ventured, nothing gained." Ever driven
and relishing challenge, he "kept his ear
to the ground" for new and promising
opportunities. As business profits rolled
in and his original bank stock and credit
lines continued appreciating, he explored
all prospects that came his way. During the
time the Italian food distribution business
was steadily advancing to nation-wide

levels, he also made several other wise investments—in upscale residential real estate and commercial land development in California, Florida and the Southwest; in minerals; timber and forest products; Pennsylvania properties with pumping oil wells; vineyards in the New York State Finger Lakes region; trucking and small rail lines; and several coal mining sites which he outfitted with state-of-the-art technology for supplying coke to the steel industry and fuel to emerging energy companies.

Often these diverse ventures involved demanding travel away from home, but Federico was virtually tireless and insensitive to hard work or mental fatigue. Indeed, his *modus operandi* was a somewhat curious but remarkably successful blend of the values of traditional capitalism and the rigors of the Protestant Ethic: the marriage of hard assets—land and natural resources— to personal ambition, careful planning and disciplined effort.

Once, in his presence, a competitor compared his many operations to a giant octopus, with tentacles reaching into practically every sphere of activity. Federico was not offended—it had a great element of truth. He knew full well, however, the sacrifices he had made and the risks he had taken to succeed, not to mention Rosalia's loving and supportive role in raising the children and maintaining the household, especially during his frequent absences.

At the time, Federico had chuckled to himself about the rather apt imagery the rival had chosen. He recalled that when he was a very young boy, a fisherman had told him that, of all the creatures in the sea, the octopus was unusually intelligent, possessing an uncanny ability to seek out hidden morsels to sustain itself.

After Rosalia's premature death, Federico had immersed himself ever more frenetically in his business affairs, as a distraction from his sorrow and loneliness at first, but then, as an all-consuming obsession to leave his family a vast and secure patrimony of sustainable, perpetual wealth. A child, grandchild, or for that matter, a never-to-be-known descendant, bereft of the comfort of money, a "financial orphan," he would not contemplate.

Unquestionably, Federico had a Midas touch. His great diversification made him practically invulnerable to shifting political and economic tides, including the Crash of '29. Even the land bust and natural disasters in the new developing areas did not impede the progress of his wide-ranging portfolio by much. The unprecedented demands for armaments and other equipment during hostilities promoted his investments in coke and minerals. Setbacks were merely temporary for the importation of food products, in part the result of the need to refit ocean-going commercial cargo liners and even some large pleasure ships for military uses. In these times of conflict, imposed governmental survival stratagems—such as food rationing for civilian populations and heightened demand for military food provisions—ended in a kind of trade-off for businesses such as Federico's. Clearly, in his manner of positive reasoning, the prudent course, in some instances, was not to wait out the uncertainties of particular markets, but rather to redeploy certain assets to promote new ventures and make-up for any real or potential losses.

By his late middle years, Federico's many thriving interests and acquisitions constituted the core of a giant holding company traded publicly on the stock exchange. Federico titled the conglomerate, "Trinacria Enterprises International, Inc.," after the ancient name of his beloved island. Expectedly, this introduced massive new capital for exponential expansion of existing assets and the development of several new ones. Eventually, this complex financial empire enabled him to create generous trusts for every member of the family and a stream of wealth for generations thereafter. At the same time, however, it also necessitated a move away from predominant family control of policy and decision-making to much greater fiduciary corporate governance. Such a transition meant, in essence, that Federico had less and less of an active role to play. Now merely as honorary chairman of the board and nearing eighty-one, it was really Fabrizio, in his mid- fifties, not he, who had to oversee and coordinate the diverse activities of the several executive officers and managers of the subsidiary or affiliate companies. For greater efficiency and profitability, some operations, in fact, were transferred to secondary headquarters in Chicago.

Out of habit, Federico would go to his office each day, even though there was really little he could do, except now and then give a nod to some minor proposal or *fait accompli*. He began to feel rather useless, like a withered or spent bloom clinging to its twig. When he suffered a minor stroke, fortunately no real serious impairment resulted, other than chronic fatigue. However, he began to admit, to himself and others close to him, that he felt his life was subsiding. Somewhat dispirited, he nevertheless persevered, with one important exception to his independence and self-reliance—driving. His physician advised strongly against it; so Chad, the caretaker and general handyman, who for decades had lived in the carriage house and was himself now in his late middle years, assumed the extra duties of maintaining his towncar and acting as his driver.

Federico had lived alone in the
big house for many years after Rosalia's
death. Cecilia, his loving and dutiful
daughter-in-law, came by to visit almost
every other day or, at the least, checked in
by phone with Rina as to his condition and
spirits. Federico looked forward to her
visits. He loved her dearly, for her blithe
and cheery disposition, her life-affirming
spirituality, and for the handsome, upright
grandsons she had given him. He knew
how much she had to put up with Fabrizio,
who, though a good-hearted man, could
be peevish and difficult and sometimes,
downright unreasonable.

Rina, the housekeeper, was also
getting on in years, but she felt a strong
and deep sense of loyalty to Federico.
When some of her relatives proposed that
she retire and join them out west, she flatly
refused, saying, "My home has always

been here. I wouldn't *think* of leaving Mister D'Argenti!"

One afternoon when Federico returned from his office, he complained to Rina that he had a headache. Taking some medicine and a glass of water, he headed for the library. Shortly thereafter, Cecilia appeared at the back door. As was her custom, she had parked her car near the rear service entrance close to the kitchen. Upon entering, she saw Rina at the sink washing dishes. "How is Papa Fede today, Rina?" she asked. "Oh, he came home complaining of a little headache. He's in the library reading or watching TV, I think."

Cecilia approached the library. Her warm "Good afternoon, Dad" had no response. Federico appeared to be sleeping. Slightly slumped in his wingchair, his worn copy of Dante in his lap, two fingers of his left hand lightly holding his bookmark, the memorial card of his beloved Rosalia— *Federico was dead.*

The Neapolitan gypsy's prediction of long ago had been fulfilled beyond measure: "Remember, young gallant—I tell you, as you get older and older, you will get richer and richer."

In the months that followed, Fabrizio, as executor, and Christopher addressed the many details of settling the immense estate. Some entailed the usual, expected things. However, there were troublesome nuances in clauses and features of Federico's complex will, even though he had consulted on a regular basis with his team of financial advisors and accountants. Fortunately, these issues were eventually resolved with the most carefully defined financial entities, the individual trusts, absolutely secure. They ensured each of the surviving members of the family huge initial outright sums of cash, numberless stocks, as well as long-term annuity incomes in the many millions of dollars.

Federico had also designated a number of charities, especially those close to Rosalia's heart and Giulietta's religious mission, as beneficiaries in perpetuity in the family foundation.

Although he had been averse to unions and their potential abuses, Federico was a humane, fair-minded and just man; he had pioneered ways for job and income security, as well as generous profit-sharing for his employees, at every level.

In the business community, Federico left an impressive and lasting legacy. At the funeral services, one of his longtime associates ended his tribute with these remarks—

"Our dear friend, Federico, was an exemplary human being, a remarkable self-made entrepreneur. Those of us fortunate to work with him recognized his extraordinary natural talents, genius and vision. I must admit, however, that I was sometimes a bit envious of that irresistible combination of good looks, unmatchable courtesy and beguiling accent with which he could disarm a competitor or captivate a prospect, or, as they say, 'Charm a snake' or 'Sell snow to the Eskimos.' All of us in the business community are going to miss his presence very much.

They say that Destiny has two faces: one that smiles, the other that frowns. Gratefully, for many years, we in the business community have been looked upon with favor, enjoying professional association and, in many instances, personal friendship with Federico. We shall miss his singular and distinguished presence very much."

In the weeks following, expressions of condolence and tribute would come from many others, both in the United States and from abroad.

DIAMONDS   As much as he had
1966   resisted his father as a young boy, Fabrizio became more like him as he matured into middle age. Although falling short of Federico's natural polish and charming and respected silver word, his business persona was still considerable—informed, cordial, reserved and evenly balanced, quite the opposite of his cranky, and sometime very melancholy behavior at home, all too familiar to his patient and understanding wife, Cecilia.

To his credit, Fabrizio had a penchant for the new, a definite flair for innovative ventures. If he wasn't surveying the financial pages, he was opening his phone lines and office to all types of individuals and aspiring little emerging companies, bona fide and wannabe, anxious to do business or soliciting seed money for some operation or another. Most of these he dismissed, but one afternoon he was visited by a middle-aged gentleman who came on a recommendation from a trusted business associate. The man's name was Earl Woodward, a geologist by training, an adventurer by disposition.

After some brief chit-chat, Woodward cut to the quick—the purpose of his visit. He said, "Mister D'Argenti, a few months ago, I visited Guyana. As is my custom, I did a little exploring. On a hunch, I discovered a huge gem vein in which, on some preliminary testing, I was able to determine there could well be diamonds of the highest quality." Pushing back in his chair and asking permission to light a cigarette, he went on to say – "I'm pretty certain that there is enough under the earth there to yield an astonishing quantity of high-grade gems, but I have no personal resources. Would you be willing to underwrite the project? I have contacts that have assured me of speedy government approvals and attractive development and tax incentives."

Woodward had an easy air of confidence and spoke with a certain authority, but Fabrizio was too practiced and clever a businessman by now to be easily taken in by any con artist. Politely, he said he was very intrigued by this proposal and that he would give it some serious consideration. Within a couple weeks, as promised, Woodward sent him all the details of his research. He also outlined, in rough fashion, the equipment that would have to be ordered and the type of initial labor force needed.

Fabrizio studied the materials thoroughly and consulted discreetly with some other tech-savvy gem experts and one of his vice-presidents in charge of research and development. Soon after, he called Mister Woodward, said the answer was "yes," and asked when it all could begin. He said he would probably assign his son, Christopher, to oversee the initiation of the project, together with some other staff people from Trinacria.

Before the next month was out, Christopher flew with Woodward and his skeletal team, first to the nearest large urban area and then, by small plane, to an airstrip close to the more remote spot, the proposed mining location. The weather patterns were at their worst, but they were nevertheless successful in arranging for the transport and eventual delivery of the heavy equipment that had been ordered, as well as the hiring of some workers.

Within a few months, the project was well underway and the results were far beyond expectation. "I guess we're literally adding a big jewel to Trinacria

Enterprises's crown, aren't we son?"
Fabrizio boasted to Christopher.

And then it happened. Christopher chose to make a brief reconnaissance trip. The small plane bringing him close to the site crashed into a low mountain. For two days, medical search and rescue teams were unable to get through the thicket of the jungle, not knowing if there were any survivors that could still be saved.

Upon hearing the awful news, Cecilia was frantic and completely beside herself. Fabrizio immediately hired a private plane out of Pittsburgh, and within a few hours, he and Cynthia, Christopher's wife, departed for Guyana. Upon their arrival, they were informed that the remains of the plane had been found, that the pilot and three passengers, including Mister Woodward, had died, and that Christopher, miraculously, was alive but severely injured. His legs had been crushed. He would never be able to walk without prosthetic devices and would often have to be confined to a wheelchair.

For a long time, Fabrizio struggled with a terrible burden of guilt. Somehow he felt responsible for his son's misfortune, that the jewel Trinacria Enterprises had gained came at too great a price.

Part Three
1968 - 1969

DECISION   As expected,   Orlando had
   1968   been deeply saddened by
Federico's death, perhaps in some ways much
more so than any of the other family members.
He fondly remembered that as a child and
into young manhood, he had enjoyed a
special, close and loving relationship with
his grandfather who delighted in telling
him about his early life and the land of his
origin, Sicily.

It has been said that "the son
may wish to remember what the father
may wish to forget." Typically, in the
immigration experience, the generation
facing the problem of social acceptance

and "fitting in," may choose or be forced to reject the past, whereas the succeeding generations, assimilated and secure, may wish to recapture it: the now familiar story of "the search for roots." Orlando was definitely of this latter mind-set, but as yet had not acted on it.

After completing his studies in architecture, he had moved to New York and purchased an apartment in a fashionable section of Manhattan. Granted, even though he wasn't under any pressure to earn money, he nevertheless took a part-time position as a lecturer in classical Greek and Roman literature at the Fordham University Rose Hill campus in the Bronx by day, and offered a course on contemporary architecture at a leading school of design on the Upper East Side, three evenings a week. Although he had studied Italian (as well as Latin and Greek) both in high school and college, he also decided to brush up on his conversational

210

ability and sat in as an audit in some courses at the beautiful Jesuit complex.

When the spring semester concluded, Orlando moved quickly on his decision to visit Sicily. It was something he regretted he hadn't done when his grandfather was alive so that he could have shared so much with him about his sojourn and his impressions. In a note to his mother, telling her about his anticipated trip, he said – "There's no excuse, Mom. I've become more and more interested in learning first-hand about baroque architecture for which Sicily is quite famous. Just recently, I read that Grandpa Fede's Noto can, in fact, be considered the 'capital city' of Sicilian baroque!"

Of course, it was clearly more than the interests of his professional calling motivating Orlando to travel to Sicily. Deep in his heart, he hoped to recapture something of the early years and experiences of his beloved grandfather who, in so many ways, was the grand architect of the D'Argenti family. More than Orlando could ever imagine, however, Grandpa Fede was going to be the architect of *his* individual future destiny as well.

CATANIA 1968   Orlando's plane landed in Catania, a large, bustling city with an international airport and close to Grandpa Fede's native Noto, reachable by way of a short and scenic drive away to the south. It was Sunday. After booking in a small hotel, Orlando was anxious to see some of the sights, leaving the matter of a car rental and other details until the next day.

While strolling the city's beautiful public garden dedicated to the memory of its famous son, opera composer Vincenzo Bellini, his attention was drawn to the attractive marble busts of literary and historical figures set artfully amidst the greenery of the major path or walkway. As he neared one of these, that of the poet Stesichorus (or *Stesicoro* in Italian), he saw three very fair young women fast approaching. Although somewhat reticent and shy in unstructured public situations, he was so taken with their extraordinary loveliness that he began spontaneously to recite aloud some apt lines from this ancient lyric poet—

"It is time to sing...

Take out the flute...

And recall the songs

Of our blond Graces..."

With a look of utter surprise, one of the women returned in perfect English – "Very impressive, *signore*, but you're probably just quoting what you memorized from the park's brochure." Laughing, Orlando replied, "I hope not. I'm supposed to know these things by heart" "Why is that?" they said in chorus.

"Oh, I probably couldn't convince you that I'm telling the truth." "Try us," one flirtatiously retorted. Pretending not to hear, he quickly asked – "How is it you speak the "Queen's English" so perfectly? Are you English?" "No, we're one hundred per cent Sicilian," one said. "The answer is simple – we had an English nanny and when we were teenagers our parents sent us for extended stays in London to study the language." Then pointing to one of her sisters, she said "Sabina lived there for over a year while doing research at the Courtauld. She's a painter."

While carrying on with this light banter, Orlando's attention was taken with the arresting beauty of these real, live "Three Graces." They appeared to be in their early or mid-twenties, all of them of the Norman Sicilian physical type. One particularly had his eye: the painter. In the very first moment he looked at her, she seemed a radiant sylph from some

Sicilian golden age. Or was she perhaps a concealed angel? At the sound of her lovely sweet, melting voice, how could he not believe it so? In an instant, Cupid's fiery arrow hit its mark – Orlando was smitten.

Like her sisters, Sabina was slender and statuesque, with lustrous blond hair, blue eyes and skin so white it looked like Parian marble. Her features rivaled the idealized beauty of an ancient statue. Of the three, however, only her countenance had that mystical, slow and dreamy smile as rendered by Leonardo in his sublime drawings of youths and angels and in his enchanting paintings of the Virgin Mary and her mother, Saint Anne.

Her sisters, he learned, were Lucia and Agata, named after the two most revered Sicilian martyr-saints. They told him that their mother had passed away recently and that they were still at home with their father, a professor of history at the university. As the conversation continued, they said they were headed for a gelato shop nearby, famous for its unique and fanciful confections. "Would you like to join us?" they asked.

Before long, Orlando found himself seated with the captivating trio at an outdoor café table with a breathtaking view of a magnificent baroque church across the narrow street. While they all enjoyed creamy pistachio gelatos made— as the attentive and ebullient shop's proprietor boasted—with nuts from choice trees on the slopes of Mount Etna, Orlando disclosed his reasons for coming to Sicily— his interest in the island's architecture and his desire to trace his grandfather's footsteps and find the palace where he had spent his early life. He referred to it as a mission, but Lucia was quick to suggest that it was more of a pilgrimage.

Before departing, Sabina asked Orlando if he would like to meet their father, someone, she thought, who could be very helpful to him. Of course, he agreed without hesitation. He had been trying desperately to think of some way to see her again.

It was mid-morning of the next day when Sabina picked Orlando up at his hotel and took him home to meet her father, Professor Lorenzo Altavilla. They seemed to share so much in common, it came as no surprise that they took to each other immediately. In the days and months following, the affable professor would be a great resource for Orlando regarding many aspects of Sicily's history and culture.

Sabina's sisters were aware of that magical something that can happen suddenly between two people. They purposely stayed in the background, confiding to their father—"Sabina is in love with Orlando. *And*, we know he is in love with her!"

It was the truth. From that very first day, they became inseparable.

THE PALACE   Orlando and Sabina 1969 would never forget their first visit to the palace, once the home of Prince Fabrizio Bronte. The directions Sabina's father had provided brought them to the terminus of one of the slopes spanning the entire breadth of the city. It was accessed by way of a major arterial road, originally platted in local scholar, G.B. Landolina's master plan to rebuild Noto *de novo*, shortly after the great earthquake of 1693. It was highly probable that the final part of this long boulevard had once constituted the approach road to the prince's palace. Now, however, it was lined on each side with modest apartment buildings, many of which sported, rather incongruously, the latest of the mid-twentieth century's technological gadgets: the ugly TV antenna.

The huge and imposing domicile of the prince sat squarely on the perpendicular, closing or blocking off the end of the road. Interestingly, its location gave it a rather unique dual personality—that of an urban palace as well as a suburban villa. It was neither hemmed in by other public buildings, as the grand Ducezio Palace in the center of Noto, nor perched all alone on a hill in the countryside, like a villa in Bagheria, south of Palermo.

Its immense rear garden (or now, only the vestiges thereof) opened to a sweeping vista, much the same as some early Roman Renaissance palaces once looked toward the Campagna.

Despite the fact that the palace had miraculously escaped any direct damage during the hostilities, the stucco and stone exterior was nevertheless in a pitiable state of dilapidation and ruin. It was overgrown with weeds and bushes that had become the size of trees; huge dangling bird nests; broken or missing shutters; and windows smashed or entirely missing, allowing the elements to penetrate into the interior. The main block or *corps de logis* was completely free of graffiti, but the service wings that had once housed offices, staff quarters (including Grandpa Fede's little room), storage areas and several elegant carriages, had not fared as well.

Under this canopy of wild growth and debris, the design was nevertheless clearly perceptible. It was a grand and impressive pile, no doubt in its prime capable of inspiring both deferential awe and envy. Although built in the enthusiastically embraced baroque style after the devastating earthquake, it had a certain unusual formalism, or restraint and *gravitas*, suggesting still other possible Roman or French influences. Some initial research by Professor Altavilla had disclosed that it was built by one of the leading baroque architects of the period, Vincenzo Sinatra, who, with Francesco Paolo Labisi, had also constructed the magnificent Ducezio Palace in Noto's center.

One of the palace's greatest assets, now however dimmed or damaged by moss, soot and other accretions, was its decorative diamond-cut stone, a variety quarried in the vicinity to the north and only to be seen in Noto. It was of an unusual pale, golden-yellow color which, when touched by sunlight, took on a mellow, amber-like richness.

The dominant horizontal aspect of the building's front elevation, achieved by the thirteen or so tall, evenly spaced pedimented windows on the *piano nobile* level, conveyed a sense of power and authority. At the same time, the delicate balconies under each window, rendered in the unique Sicilian manner, bestowed a sense or feeling of lightness and gaiety. At the attic level, just under the roof cornice, several large symmetrically placed classical motifs or studies in high relief, also gave the façade a fascinating animated and expressive elegance.

Without question, however, the most impressive baroque feature of the façade was the ingenious pincer-shaped staircase that swept up from two sides and arrived at an enormous curvilinear entry. The massive double-door, with its elaborately carved surround, was topped by a scalloped-shaped cartouche, rubbed smooth by time and the elements. At each side of the building, left and right front, was affixed a monumental, storey-high carved stone volute, seeming to anchor or rather bookend the huge structure.

The palace's long and straight dependencies or service wings differed from other accepted or popular styles, such as the curvaceous, horseshoe-shaped designs of Tommaso Napoli at Villa Valguarnera in Bagheria, or Mario Gioffredo's totally open colonnaded treatment (in the manner of Bernini at Saint Peter's in Rome) at Villa Campolieto along the "golden mile" of the royal Vesuvian road on the Italian mainland. Interestingly, Sinatra's contrasting schema set strict rectilinear boundaries to the palace's immense forecourt, the pavement of which, barely visible, was composed of a swirling pattern of small, pebble-like white stones and yellow flint set in dark lava. In imitation of Antonio Carnevari's "Reggia" or royal summer palace of the Bourbons at Portici, outside of Naples, the Sicilian architect enclosed these annexes, thereby providing a great amount of internal space or rooms for diverse uses.

The tiled flat tops or roofs of these functional appendages once constituted elegant promenade terraces, enclosed with balustrades and stands or pedestals on which marble portrait busts rested or presided. These adornments were now either broken beyond recognition or entirely missing.

As they travelled through the town on their way to the palace, Orlando had recognized some of the places his grandfather had often described to him. For the most part, they were still there unchanged, except for the wear of the years, or in some cases, benign neglect. Sabina could detect Orlando's joy by the look on his face and the enthusiasm of his voice.

It was very different when they worked their way past the huge gnarled and rusted gate to the prince's palace. For a minute or two, Orlando seemed transfixed and lost in thought. Sabina sensed that something extraordinary was happening and she placed her hand lightly on his shoulder. Tilting his head back slightly, as if awakening or emerging from a rapture, Orlando then said, in a soft, impassioned voice—

"You know, Sabina, there's nothing more challenging and gratifying for an architect than to take a beautiful but moribund building and breathe new life into it. I want to do just that with this magnificent structure. With you at my side, with your understanding and help, it will give me the greatest satisfaction and happiness." Then, in a deeper register and with a more pensive look, he opined—

"Somehow, I believe too that I will, in some way, redeem the nostalgia my grandfather had for Sicily and the deep claim the memories of his early experiences in Noto and at this palace had on him in his twilight years. No matter how successful he was in America, I always felt that he had a longing for the place of his youth. Strangely, he never proposed to revisit here. Perhaps it would have been too painful. What it might have recalled—especially the memories of my grandmother, Rosalia, whom he adored and missed terribly—would have been truly bittersweet."

With an approving look, Sabina said simply – "*Amore*, let me help you do it."

Part Four
1969 - 1971

RESTORATION   About   two   months
  1969-1971   later,   once Orlando
had succeeded in maneuvering through
a number of bureaucratic obstacles with
Professor Altavilla's help, he and Sabina
were finally permitted to enter the palace
in the company of an appointed town
official.

Despite the fact that, for years,
rain and winds had penetrated the interior,
the degree of damage was surprisingly
not as radical or cataclysmic as expected.
Unfortunately, nevertheless, what had
taken place was a slow but persistent
process of disintegration of *rococo* stucco

decorations of garlands and festoons of leaves and flowers, shells and wistful *amorini* adorning door surrounds, friezes, columns, giant pilasters and moldings of diverse designs. Immediately apparent, as well, was the fading or peeling away of enchanting frescoes and murals, and many costly silk wall coverings, the shredded, thread-bare vestiges of which now faintly hinted of their former beautiful colorings of subtle ice blues, quiet greys and greens, soft yellows and brilliant crimson reds.

All the window treatments, short of a few extraordinary wood lambrequins, painted to resemble fabric with tassels and lace, had also completely decomposed. Perhaps worst of all, the furnishings—with the exception of a lonely, tattered borne or large pouf still in the center of one or two of the salons or drawingrooms—had vanished.

Given the tastes and customs of the period, one could also assume that several elegant vitrines would have been among the appointments of these aristocratic rooms. Sadly, they too were gone and all their precious content of rare porcelains and other *objets d'art* which, once securely locked behind glass, were believed, mistakenly, to be safely shielded from the tempests of a rude and unworthy outside world.

Some broken colored glass, here and there on the charming terracotta, majolica tile and costly marble floors, suggested that incidents of vandalism may also have been the unfortunate fate of several spectacular chandeliers or very tall crystal candelabra.

At some distance from where they had entered—the majestic and awe-inspiring rotunda—Orlando and Sabina proceeded with their guide down one of several long mirrored hallways, coming upon a large rectangular chamber, a billiards or game room, with intricately carved pole bracket stands, a moth-eaten banquette that once seated players and observers, and a large rusted lantern dangling from a metal tray ceiling with a wide concave molding ornamented with colorful but somewhat faded armorial and heraldic crests.

Within a short distance from this masculine retreat, they approached a truly remarkable room which would come to hold Orlando's greatest interest—the library. Neoclassical in design—with a high and undecorated white barrel-vaulted ceiling, supported by a single, tall Ionic column in each corner—it stood in sharp, rather chaste, contrast to the many more ornate architectural elements in the rest of the palace.

Its still discernible color palette was unusual and most attractive. Against the paneled walls of walnut, the bi-level glazed bookcases were painted in a subdued matte Pompeian red and decorated with stenciled Greco-Roman grotesques in muted black-grey and bluish pewter. The intact and massive chandelier in the center of the room was of intricate wrought-iron and finished in the same colors, with just a hint or trace of silver.

Orlando's attention was quickly drawn to two tall niches, one centered at each far end-wall of this fascinating room. A rusted iron bracket in one suggested that these recesses had once held large vases, most likely, antique amphorae.

Ever the scholar, Orlando could not help but wonder what treasures had once graced the shelves of this learned sanctum. In his mind's eye, he pictured rare and precious antique Greek, Roman and Arabic tracts and manuscripts and early printed works on the subjects dear to the prince's questing intellect and interests—astronomy, art, archaeology, natural history, music, mythology and drama—as well as luxuriously embossed and gilded leather-bound volumes of *belles-lettres*.

(Sometime later, Orlando's examination of extant public records and other more informal sleuthing would confirm what he had initially suspected—that many things had been sold or relinquished to compensate creditors, particularly if the prince had failed to include them in his codicil. However, to his relief and delight, he also learned that the nobleman had willed most of his library collection to the University of Palermo. Fortunately, some old photographs of the palace's interior, discovered folded or pressed in pages of these books, would eventually become available to Sabina and be especially helpful in her attempt to recreate the original ambience of several of the rooms.)

When the friendly town official threw open the shutters to the smaller of the two dining rooms, Sabina was astonished. This morning room, where the prince and his family would have gathered privately and more informally, had a most creative design and decoration. It was circular in shape, with a spherical or cupola-like ceiling. With the mind and hand of an illustrator of sacred books, or a decorator of some exquisite illuminated medieval or Renaissance Book of Hours, the muralist had delicately rendered vines and ivy draping from the ceiling's center right down to the trellise-like wainscoting, placing here and there, exotic, colorful birds and unusual blossoms and flowers. Although faded and partially damaged, the total effect was that of a magical garden pergola or some dream-like pavilion straight out of the "Arabian Nights." Even though it was one of the smallest of the palace's main rooms, Sabina would come to consider it, by far, the most enchanting.

The adornment of the large dining room differed to a great degree from that of the adjacent grand ballroom. It had many beautiful stucco decorations (sorely in need of restoration), relatively intact striated black and white marble flooring and an intricately coffered rose-colored ceiling accented with heavy silverleaf. Given this color schema and the pieces of glass scattered on the floor, Sabina and Orlando surmised that the several chandeliers, now gone, would have been of opalescent and deep-rose Venetian glass. Several large, rusty hooks and the remnants of wiring and ribbons on the walls suggested that paintings—perhaps still-lifes, classical subjects or portraits of ancestors—may have constituted the principal decoration of this enormous banqueting room.

The walls of the ballroom, on the other hand, had been entirely mirrored with sumptuous overlay of brilliantly gilded stucco arabesques. Its ceiling painting, an oval fresco of a luminous peach and blue sky, with darting *putti* attending graceful, crowned female figures representing the Virtues (among them, Charity, Prudence, Magnanimity and Justice), grandly celebrated the motto of the Terranova-Chiaravalle lineage— "Secure in virtue."

In a moment of reverie, Sabina imagined how many, many years before, the jewels of the ladies dancing in this candlelit room would have seemed pulsating stars in the midnight firmament or flickering pearlescent lights on the surfaces of a dark and glassy sea. Her later research on the elements of the room would reveal that the depiction of the radiant Virtues was inspired, in part, by the *Iconologia* (or Iconology) of Cesare Ripa, published as early as 1603.

Sadly, the several chandeliers of this spectacular room were also all missing, but miraculously, the unusual azure and yellow majolica flooring was virtually intact and only in need of cleaning and polishing. The intricately rendered gilded railing, enclosing the small, slightly elevated orchestra gallery, was broken in several places and would require the skill of an exceptionally talented smith to restore it.

Each of the several high-ceilinged drawing rooms and their anterooms—all linked on an axis—featured a single primary color scheme: blue, red or yellow, deftly blended in derivative shades and hues. In all likelihood, it was the blue room, distinguished by its whimsical musical motifs in stucco, to which Prince Bronte would have often retreated to play his treasured harpsichord. The floors of all these rooms were of intricate parquet, now in need of extensive refinishing.

One little anteroom, however, stood out from the rest. It was a *gabinetto in porcellana*, a room rendered in porcelain *chinoiserie*, a costly decorative style quite popular among the gentry who chose to emulate the tastes and fashions of the sovereigns. Orlando quickly recognized the vestibule's probable connection to the fantastic oriental architectural folly, "La Favorita," which Sabina and her father had taken him to see on a tour of the sights of Palermo. Sometime later, when they had determined that the unique room's elements had been fashioned at the royal Capodimonte factory in Naples, a porcelain manufactory remarkably still in operation after three centuries, they agreed that they would eventually need to consult there for any proper restoration.

The enormous loggia spanning the entire rear of the palace block overlooked what once had been a carefully tended formal garden, a vast plateau, now still beautifully framed on each side by long-unattended, but nevertheless miraculously thriving flowering almond trees. Happily, the deep and sweeping vista to the distant sea beyond, remained unmarred by any intervening or encroaching later-day eyesores. Although the delicately frescoed walls and ceiling of the loggia had paled and dimmed, Orlando could still identify or interpret the classical epigrams, allegorical themes and pastoral subjects depicted.

For Sabina, who loved flowers and tending them, it was particularly painful to see that the once bright and colorful southern flora, as well as many varieties of rare cacti and palms of the prince's former garden, were now choked beyond recognition in an almost impenetrable tangle of their own overgrowth. The many statues that had adorned the garden were gone; only fragments and some bases remained, in place or toppled and barely visible under the unbridled vegetation. Somewhat like the people who once inhabited the palace, their individual identities and significances were obscured or lost by indifferent nature and the pitiless march of time.

Some quick, on-the-spot mental calculations convinced Orlando that the repair of the palace's roof would be one of the costliest expenditures. The old wine-soaked tiles would need to be set aside, to be returned to their places only after the massive truss substructure was either reinforced or entirely rebuilt.

Of course, all the basic facilities— plumbing, heating and electrical systems— were antiquated and needed either modern adaptation or total replacement. With just a few exceptions, the many fireplaces and over-mantels of varying designs, were merely soiled or discolored but otherwise undamaged. However, installation of modern duct and air conditioning systems would require extensive intervention with very expensive technical labor and materials.

Without question, the repair or replacement of the palace's many windows would be of first-order importance, thereby preventing any further damage to the interior or any initial restoration efforts.

The challenge of bringing the palace to its former glory was intimidating, to say the least. Yet, Orlando, like his childhood hero, Roland the Crusader, was undaunted and determined to succeed. He fondly recalled his grandfather's wise observation and comment from long ago, when his dad found fault with him: "Why not let the boy follow his loves and interests? In the end, that brings true happiness and success."

At the moment, the cost in time, talent and effort—as well as unforeseen problems and frustrations—was incalculable; the cost in hard currency, undoubtedly, would be in the range of several million dollars.

It was an endeavor, however, which he would enjoy with the love of his life, Sabina. Above everything else, he was especially delighted and encouraged by the fact that they shared an aesthetic sensibility and she found the renewal of the palace a veritable bouquet for her artistic imagination. Musing perhaps a little extravagantly, Orlando thought that Lord and Lady Elgin could not have enjoyed more satisfaction and pride in their rescue of the treasures of Periclean Greece than he and Sabina would experience in this undertaking. True, it was extremely modest by any measure of comparison, but it was something that nevertheless held inestimable personal and sentimental value.

Just the thought—that as a little boy, his beloved grandfather had once played along the paths of these dependencies, perhaps sometime chasing a butterfly or a little rabbit into the prince's garden, and listened wide-eyed to many of Mariannina's enchanting stories under the shade of one of these porticoes; or later, as a young man, had dreamed of his future life with his love, Rosalia, as he fell off to sleep in his little service wing room—was incentive enough for Orlando to go forward with eagerness and enthusiasm.

In all, it would take more than forty able and talented workmen—master masons, carpenters, smiths, plumbers, electricians, artisans (in fabrics, tile, mosaic and stucco), gilders, muralists, antiquarians, gardeners and landscapers, and many other specialists, engaged more than ten to twelve hours a day, for the next fourteen to fifteen months—to bring the basic restoration close to completion.

Orlando and Sabina would work together every day, in constant consultation with their chief contractor and his several subordinate supervisors, the workmen and all the specialists—she, concentrating more on the aesthetic aspects; and he, initially, the engineering and structural issues. Professor Altavilla also would "stand at the ready" to research something of interest or to give an informed opinion.

Even after the formal public opening of the many rooms of the *piano nobile* and the rear loggia with its beautifully reconstituted formal garden, there would remain three or four major "works-in-progress": the restoration and refurbishment of the small theater, the family chapel (in which only the elaborate baroque polychrome marble altar was still intact), the prince's small rooftop observatory, and a number of the bedrooms in the *foresteria* or guest section of the palace.

Over the years, it would be their goal—perhaps more so Sabina's—to recreate the ambience of the interior as it might have been close to the turn of the century. Early on, they would comb all the antique shops, flea markets and galleries of the island and Naples, as well as other mainland cities such as Rome, Florence and Venice, hoping to discover and reclaim authentic pieces from the prince's dispersed treasure.

During business or pleasure trips to London, Paris and New York (where they maintained Orlando's spacious original apartment), they would never fail to do likewise. They would also regularly attend auctions to purchase furniture, paintings, china and silver services, clocks, tapestries, porcelains and many other *objets d'art* and *cose adorne*, that is, precious things stamped uniquely with the personality of a specific artisan or collector.

Remarkably, on one of their earliest excursions into Naples, they would stumble upon a wonderful find in a dim corner of a cluttered and dusty antique shop off the once stately Via Toledo: a beautiful portrait

244

of the prince's maternal great-grandmother. Seated on an elaborate gilt *fauteuil*, she was bejeweled and held a delicately painted fan as she looked directly and serenely at the viewer. They may easily have passed over the picture had not the portraitist painted the family coat of arms in the upper left-hand corner of the picture: a red and gold shield blazoned with a tall, crenellated tower at its center, flanked by an olive tree on each side, and topped with a scroll inscribed with the motto, *"Virtute securus,"* supported by a pair of fearsome hippogriffs. On the back of the painting, a very faint, undated inscription read -- "Maria Elena of the Duchy Lo Faso, Sicilia."

From the very beginning, it was not unusual for dealers or connoisseurs to appear unannounced at the doorstep with an object of interest or a promising lead for some treasure. One rather bizarre and amusing such incident took place one morning when Orlando came upon a well-known antique dealer fast asleep in an ornate astronomer's chair, right in the middle of the palace courtyard!

From the inaugural period and thereafter, a visitor's leisurely progress or tour—from the palace gate and forecourt, to the ascent of the sweeping staircase, entry into the grand rotunda, passage through the enfilade of gorgeous rooms, and finally on to the spectacular vista from the garden loggia—would be nothing less than a *"promenade majesté,"* a stroll capable of taking one's breath away and transporting one to the magic and elegance of another time.

AN ANNOUNCEMENT 1969	Over several months, Orlando had sent postcards

and brief notes to his parents, never once

revealing to them his intention of remaining in Sicily and restoring the palace of the prince. When "all was go," however, and he was certain that he could realize his aim, he sat down and wrote a long letter to his mother. She always understood and supported him. Certainly, he was an independent adult now. He really didn't need his parents' approval, but he wanted to share many things, particularly the most important of all, his love for Sabina and his plan to marry her.

When Cecilia received his letter, she sensed by its tone that not only had he found his true love but, with his plan to restore the palace, he had a project that would give him a sense of purpose and fulfillment. With a mother's intuition and a good measure of that Celtic mystical understanding or grasp of things, she knew that he had needed an expressive focus or creative center and now had found it. She was thrilled to know that he was finally going to drink from the cup of life more fully. To her thinking, the excitement and enthusiasm he was experiencing seemed to resemble his grandfather Federico's zest for life and, in her response, she told him so –

"You sound just like Papa Fede – great!" She then added –"Your description of the warmth and hospitality of the Sicilian people comes as no surprise. It's legendary, I guess, but I knew it first-hand with Grandma and Grandpa D'Argenti!"

Orlando described to her some of the practical and personal uses of the palace he envisioned. In the palace service wings, he intended to establish an architectural firm that would serve an international clientele. Sabina, he noted, hoped to create a studio for her own work and an art school with special programs for talented underprivileged children and youths from across the island.

He explained that, according to the

formal agreements he was entering with government authorities, he and Sabina would eventually take up residence in a large, modernized apartment in a converted section of the *piano nobile*, while most of the formal rooms and the restored garden would be open to the public for tours a certain number of days each month, and for occasional state and cultural functions, such as the reception of dignitaries, special musical events and the like. The formal rooms, nevertheless, would be theirs, as owners, for private purposes whenever they chose. As soon as the palace would receive accredited status as a historic landmark, he would assume the title of "Director" and Sabina "Curator of Art and Special Collections."

In a brief aside, he said that—in view of the recently acclaimed "economic miracle" taking shape and promising to place Italy among the major players of industrial nations of the future—he hoped to encourage his father and brother to consider putting private equity investments in projects or emerging enterprises to boost and advance the Sicilian economy.

After relating all these details, Orlando also assured his mother that he intended to keep his Manhattan apartment so that now and then he and Sabina could enjoy the cultural life and social scene of New York and be close to visit home, as well.

Nearing the end of his letter, Orlando observed that, under the Sicilian sun, he had come to understand and appreciate how the experiences with his beloved grandfather, his studies, and now the love and companionship of Sabina were all coming together in a deeply meaningful way. Long in the making, it was an "awakening" (as he called it), full of promise and future happiness. Putting it simply, he opined—"Sicily has been the key to understanding myself and what I really want out of life."

Then, signing off with warm expressions of love and affection, he closed with Goethe's oft-quoted apostróphe to the island:

"To have seen Italy without having seen Sicily is not to have seen Italy at all, for Sicily is the clue to everything"

"You're doing all the right things, Orlando," wrote Cecilia in response. "I'll be anxious to come to Sicily, first of all, to meet Sabina and attend your wedding, and also to see this marvelous palace. Any chance you might just drop doing things for a brief weekend and fly home so that we can give you a little party and our friends can meet Sabina?"

"Your Dad is thrilled about your proposed marriage, but as you might expect, he's not happy about your palace project. Several times, he has said to me – 'I think he's very foolish to put so much of

251

his good money into an old thing like that! But then again, it's *his* money!'" (Actually, he used other expressions Cecilia decided she wouldn't mention).

However she then added, "He is looking forward to meeting Sabina and he is coming to your wedding. *And, can you believe it? He told me to send you grandfather's gold orrery!!* Isn't that strange, Orlando? Maybe secretly he does have a soft place in his heart for what you're doing.

You noted that the palace has a beautiful library. Dad's proposal made me think that perhaps you might like me to send you Grandma Rosalia's beautiful collection of nineteenth century art books and commentaries. I can send them either with the orrery or separately. Would you let me know your thoughts? And, by the way, Aunt Giulietta told me that things have changed at the convent, and that if she can find a companion sister, they will join us to fly to Sicily. Isn't that a nice surprise? She also asked if Grandma Rosalia's convent is still in existence. She'd like very much to visit it. Can you find out or do you already know?"

Your brother, Chris, is thrilled about coming too. Cynthia has already inquired about arrangements for taking his special wheelchair on the flight."

Then, jokingly she mused – "You described how lovely Sabina is and that she has blue eyes. You have green eyes. Does that mean my grandchildren will have violet eyes like Elizabeth Taylor?"

Ending on a serious note, Cecilia wrote – "What's happening to you, darling, I know in my heart and soul, is part of God's plan for you. Embrace it with joy.

Love and Kisses, Mom.

P.S. Do send us a photo of Sabina and you!

P.P.S. Your Dad found your comments about the Sicilian

economy not only interesting but a funny coincidence. He had just read an article in one of his business journals about the Pirelli Tower in Milan touted as a symbol of the Italian "economic miracle" you mentioned. He was very intrigued by your proposal to invest in the Sicilian economy and wanted to know about the discovery of oil in Gela. Are you familiar with this?"

THE PLASTER MODELS   One of the 1970   finishing touches of the palace's restoration was the replacement of the statues of Demeter and Proserpina the prince had willed to the museum at Palermo.   Orlando fondly remembered his grandfather's oft-repeated moving account of their discovery and of their special placement and exhibition by the prince in the palace's rotunda entry.   Now the niches had been carefully refurbished and were ready to receive the beautiful images once again.

A phone call or two and a brief but rather formal letter of request, accompanied with a note of introduction from his future father-in-law, Professor Altavilla, assured Orlando of an appointment with the director of the museum and his curator of antiquities.

At the outset of the meeting, the director was polite but somewhat distant; standing nearby, his dark and handsome, impeccably attired curator was totally impassive, stone-faced—he could almost have been a statue himself. Given this rather frigid demeanor, Orlando and Sabina (who had come along to assist in conversing in Italian) expected an outright rejection of the request to have plaster models cast from the antique pieces, even though it was clearly understood that it would be entirely at Orlando's expense.

The director kept fidgeting and nervously rearranging things on his desk, seeming at times, to be deep in thought or conflicted. He then began making somewhat lame excuses, such as the potential danger of injuring the statues and the need for art historians and forensic specialists to view them for their research purposes. Sabina looked furtively at Orlando, rolling her eyes as if to say, "It's never going to happen." Then, *volte-face,* the director brightened up, smiled broadly and said— "We can do it for you, Professor D'Argenti, but it will take my specialists several months to get around to it. They are very busy now preparing other things for an international show. Can you wait?"

Sabina quietly breathed a sigh of relief. The taciturn curator, who had been sneaking admiring glances at her, forced a smile. Orlando tried to suppress the thought that the director had realized that the wealthy American sitting in front of him could very well be an important benefactor of the museum at some time in the future.

Winking at Sabina and then turning around to the director, he said solemnly— "I and the citizens of Noto will be forever grateful to you."

THE LETTER 1971   Orlando was up early this April morning for the delivery of the statues from the conservator's workshop of the Palermo museum. As he neared the drafting table and temporary desk he had set up in the midst of some final restoration work in the former study of the prince, he noticed a small packet of what appeared to be letters, loosely wrapped with a faded blue ribbon, with the initials "FBTC" and a shield delicately embossed in one corner. A scribbled note on the top of the packet read: "Professor D'Argenti – Yesterday, as we were refinishing the *intarsio* surfaces of one of the walls in the study, we found this cache of letters in a secret compartment."

Orlando fingered through the letters, astonished to discover that they were all from America—letters sent by his grandfather to the prince. He knew that, over the years, his grandfather had occasionally written to the prince, but why did the prince save them, secreting them in a special compartment? Still more curious, what was in the large, sealed embossed envelope?

As he sat down and opened it, he found a small sepia-toned picture of a refined-looking, aristocratic young woman and an undated letter, written in a very elegant hand. Beginning with an enigmatic inscription, it read…

Noto, Sicily

"Others he saved, his own
he did not"

My dear Federico,

I have attempted a letter such as this a
thousand times before and a thousand
times before I have never been able to
complete it. Over the years, I have also
hoped against hope that perhaps the wish I
had expressed when I gave you the orrery
many years ago would have come true and
that you may have returned. If that were to
have happened, I prayed that I would then
have had the courage to explain things to
you in person and have the opportunity to
rectify a great injustice for which, I am
certain, I will be severely condemned by
the Almighty.

It is a very sad story I have to relate, and
you, dear Federico, although all this
time unknown to you, have been at its
center. My adult life, beginning in my
mid-twenties, has been one of concealed,

secret mental anguish, with no one with whom I felt I could safely confide.

Before I can even admit to what I am about to reveal to you, I beg that you will have it in your heart to forgive me. This has given me much pain, but perhaps when the truth is known, I will feel free and not see my life as a lie or, God forbid, that of a fool or unrepentant hypocrite.

When I was a young man, the times—the mores and attitudes—were quite different from what they are today. People were expected to respect and abide by certain time-tested traditions and ways of behaving. To challenge them or break them was unthinkable, and if such were ever the case, the consequences were often serious, sometimes with dreadfully unhappy results.

When I was a student in Rome, I was introduced to a very beautiful young woman, Ottavia Dovizzi-Malaspini, the daughter of a count of a very ancient and powerful noble family whose male members for centuries had served the Papal Court with honor and distinction. Ottavia and I fell passionately in love and spent many wonderful times together. Our indiscretions, however, dictated a tragic and terrible solution, ending in great unhappiness for us both.

My sweet Ottavia spent her life in the confines of a convent. She is dead now, may her soul rest in peace. And I, separated from her, the love of my life, lived—despite outward appearances—a rather joyless existence here. As you may remember, I had the company of my sister and brother, now both deceased with no heirs; but I, Federico, have been, both in mind and spirit, all alone, my studies of the heavens, my music, and my philanthropies, *Deo gratias*, escapes or welcomed distractions from my grief. Even these are now all but over with my many possessions, victims of the times and other reversals, dwindling to practically nothing. Who would have thought it could ever be said of me—

"Sonam perdidit"—"He lost his purse, his fortune!"

When you were here, Federico, you brought simple joys into my life. I kept you, however, at more than arm's length, giving you the fictitious identity of a foundling abandoned at my Palermo townhouse gate. Was it to shelter my love Ottavia from scandal or was it really only my reputation I was more interested in protecting?

There may indeed have been rumours here in Noto, but they never reached my ears, or thankfully, yours. Perhaps Monsignor de Florio, of blessed memory, may indeed have had his suspicions or even known something through the channels of the church, but given his usual discreet and gentle manner, he never asked about or insinuated anything. I truly believe, however, this may have explained his constant concern and prayers for you, not only when you were here, but even after you departed so suddenly for America.

At first, I had considered entrusting you to a family of quality or to distant relatives in the north of France, but I just couldn't bear the thought of long separation or the possibility of alienating your affections forever. In retrospect, I lament the middle course I chose. It was so wrong, so contemptible. And, in the end, I thwarted joys that could have been yours, mine—ours. There has been, dear Federico, neither nepenthe to remedy my sorrow nor mask or mantle to conceal my odium.

Oh misery! Oh shame! All this time, dear Federico, I have deprived you of your true identity and heritage. The irrefutable attestation of your noble blood is inscribed in the baptismal registry of the Santa Maria Maggiore basilica in Rome.

Each time I saw you, especially as a little fellow, Federico, I saw the countenance of Ottavia, your lovely Mother. Will you ever forgive me, my son?

With a heavy heart

Your eternally remorseful Father

Fabrizio Bronte

Prince of Terranova-Chiaravalle

Stunned by the letter's revelations, Orlando sat immobile, suspended in a state of utter disbelief. Then, suddenly overwhelmed by an avalanche of emotions and memories, he broke down and wept. Upon regaining some composure, he gazed tenderly at the photograph of his grandfather's beautiful mother before returning it and the letter to the envelope.

Within a few minutes, he heard the noisy entry of a truck in the courtyard below. *As he placed the envelope next to his beloved grandfather's orrery, he gently nudged the golden mechanism, setting the tiny planets spinning into orbit.* Then, with his spirit brightening, he hastened down the long stairs to welcome Proserpina and her mother and the arrival of a splendid Sicilian spring.